Rutland Railroad Company

Heart of the Green Mountains

Rutland Railroad Company

Heart of the Green Mountains

ISBN/EAN: 9783742820051

Manufactured in Europe, USA, Canada, Australia, Japa

Cover: Foto ©Andreas Hilbeck / pixelio.de

Manufactured and distributed by brebook publishing software
(www.brebook.com)

Rutland Railroad Company

Heart of the Green Mountains

Heart of the Green Mountains

RUTLAND RAILROAD COMPANY

Souvenir Edition

SEASON OF 1897

PERCIVAL W. CLEMENT
President

H. A. HODGE
Traffic Manager

E. B. ALDRICH
General Passenger Agent

General Offices: Rutland, Vt.

Typography and Presswork
by
Rockwell and Churchill Press, Boston

Preface.

※

HE author has presumed to depart from the beaten path, and to embody in this souvenir edition not only such information as will enable those in search of health or pleasure to readily find it, but to place before them such historical facts, pertinent to the vicinity they may choose to visit, as will afford constant entertainment, musing upon the past, comparing the present, and forecasting the future.

No attempt has been made to subordinate an actuality to literary ambition or display, and the reader may confidently rely upon all the statements of fact given, to the confirmation of which much time has been devoted.

Contents.

LOCAL SKETCHES.

ADVERTISEMENTS.

Introductory.

THE line of the Rutland railroad in southern Vermont, from the Connecticut valley over the Green mountains, to the valley of the Otter and thence on to the Champlain region, is older than any historical record. First an Indian trail, then a bridle-path for white settlers, then a military road, then a turnpike and stage route, it finally becomes the course of a great railway forming an important link between the traffic systems of New England and the West. Whether as a war path of savages, or guide to the pioneer, or channel of commerce, the history of this natural highway is of absorbing interest. It runs through a country with a noble history; it carries the tourist into high altitudes where the oppressive heat of summer cannot follow, and where the mountains rich in minerals and the valleys well cultivated are a continual source of delight. In fact, it opens up a land which Nature and the Yankee have coöperated in making famous.

List of Illustrations.

Heart of the Green Mountains.

The Rutland Railroad.

UNNING as it does through the heart of the Green mountains to the valley of the Champlain, the Rutland railroad is the most picturesque line in New England. Beginning at Bellows Falls the road has an altitude of two hundred and eighty-two feet above tide water, and gradually ascends to the Summit, where the road-bed lies one thousand five hundred and twenty-seven feet above the level of the sea, making the rise from Bellows Falls nine hundred and eighty-five feet in a distance of thirty-four miles. From the Summit to Rutland, five hundred and sixty-two feet above tide water, the descent is sharp, the distance being but nineteen miles. The line from Bellows Falls to Rutland constitutes the mountain division of the road. From Rutland the line follows Otter creek northward, and at Burlington, sixty-seven miles beyond, has descended four hundred and fifty-six feet, nearly to the level of Lake Champlain, which has an altitude of ninety-six feet above the Atlantic. This stretch of track, with the Addison branch, running from Leicester Junction to Ticonderoga, N.Y., constitutes the Champlain division. So it is that passing over the road from Bellows Falls to Burlington one is brought in touch with the wildest and most romantic spots in the Green mountain range, as well as the two most fertile valleys in Vermont.

The Most Picturesque Line in New England.

The road was projected in 1843, when it was found that a portage from Lake Champlain to the Connecticut river would be of great commercial value. The first paragraph printed on this subject appeared in the "Bellows Falls Gazette" in the summer of 1843. Dr. S. M. Blake, who was at that time editor of the paper, wrote the paragraph, which resulted in a meeting of those interested in the project. It was a stupendous undertaking in those days of pioneer railroading, but the men into whose hands the enterprise had fallen strove long and faithfully, and in the end succeeded. Application for a charter was made to the Legislature, and two were ultimately granted. One was approved Nov. 1, 1843, and the other Oct. 31, 1844. These gave the line the name of the Champlain and Connecticut road. On Nov. 6, 1845, the commissioners met, and on June 10 of that year stock books were opened for subscriptions. On the third of July following the directors organized, and on Jan. 13, 1847, the first contracts were awarded. November 6 of that year the name of the road was changed to Rutland and Burlington, and on Dec. 18, 1849, the line was opened for travel. In President Follett's address, delivered before the annual stockholders' meeting, June 19, 1850, he says:

And now, gentlemen, your board have the high gratification of being able to announce to you in this formal manner, what you already know and understand, that your direction in this matter has been obeyed. A train of cars from the ocean, and another from the lake, each full freighted with stock-holders and friends of this enterprise, met and exchanged congratulations in the rock excavation upon the summit at Mount Holly, on the 18th December, 1849; being thirteen days in advance of the period when this whole work, by your order, was directed to be finished. From that day to the present, regular daily trains for freight and passengers have passed each way over the entire line. The Rutland and Burlington railroad, omitting a fraction, is

120 miles in length, forming the northwestern portion of the great trunk line from Boston to Lake Champlain, and there connecting with the various avenues leading to Canada and the western lakes. The cost of this road was estimated in its preliminary survey at $8,000,000. It was to cross the Green mountains in Vermont, at an elevation of some 1,400 feet above tide, and was to encounter, at that point especially, an obstacle in rock-cutting of a most formidable and expensive character, — too much so, in the opinion of many, to justify the necessary outlay. The contractors commenced the work of grading in the spring of 1847, since which, up to the day of its completion in December, 1849, the work progressed regularly and steadily, and with but occasional and partial interruptions. During this short period there have been removed 5,645,194 cubic yards of earth, more than 1,500,000 of which is a tenacious clay, hardpan, and quicksand; and 323,480 yards of solid and 21,999 yards of loose rock. There have been constructed 21,911½ yards of culvert masonry; 38,125¼ yards of bridge masonry; 1,297 yards of arch and pier masonry; 16,336 yards of bank and supporting wall, and 5,500¼ lineal feet of bridging. The mechanical character of this work, for durability and strength, and for architectural symmetry and beauty, will bear comparison, we think, with similar work wherever found in this country. The entire line of track, which, with necessary turnouts, does not fall short of 125 miles in length, was laid in six and a half months by one party of contractors. The sum of $24,000 has been paid for fencing, embracing a large portion of the line which passes through the cultivated parts of the country, where fencing was immediately necessary, and $17,028.17 for depot buildings, principally at way-stations.

March 28, 1867, there was a reorganization of the road, and the name was again changed, this time to the Rutland railroad, which name it bears to-day.

During the period of construction there was an increased business activity noted throughout western Vermont. This has continued to the present time. Many found employment on the road, and capitalists, finding an easy market in Boston for their manufactures, started up more than one industry. Brandon to-day owes no small part of its healthy growth to the building of car-shops there. All the cars used on the line when it was first operated were made in Brandon, and all the cast-iron work was also made there from ore procured in Brandon and Pittsford. These were the days when eighteen-ton "wood-burner" locomotives were used on the passenger trains, and when it was necessary to "wood up" twice between Rutland and the Summit, and four times between Bellows Falls and the top of the mountain.

Township of Rockingham.

THE development of modern travel by steam has made sad work with some of our civic centres. Rockingham cut a figure in early history; but one corner of that township, called Bellows Falls, now takes much of the glory, as it is an important distributing point and no mean manufacturing centre.

Five Hamlets.

Of the five villages included in Rockingham, this is now the only one of sufficient size to promote any important industry. Bellows Falls, together with Rockingham village and Bartonsville, are on the line of the Rutland railroad. The other thriving villages, Cambridgeport and Saxton's River, stowed away among the foot-hills of the Green mountains, can be reached by stage from Bellows Falls through a country affording choice bits of scenery that will well repay a visit.

An Old Town.

The written records of Rockingham date back to 1754, but the doings of the settlers very much farther; indeed, back to the times when the whites started out on the Lord's day, armed with flint-locks, and so ready to meet either the redskin or the adversary. The first inhabitants were drawn to this section by the fishing at the falls rather than by the quality of the soil, as in those days the Connecticut river swarmed with salmon on their way

A GLIMPSE OF CAVENDISH WOODS

from Long Island sound to the spawning beds near the Connecticut lakes. But though Rockingham plantation lived, the Indian warriors dwarfed the growth of the town. The settlers were a sturdy set, but few in numbers, as appeared from the count of one Joseph Blanchard, "a man of accurate calculation," who, in 1755, took a census of the families living between Rockingham and Hartford, Vt., and found not over sixty.

The Proto-
martyr
of the
Revolution.

About the middle of the eighteenth century the courts met at Chester, eight miles northwest, but as the Connecticut-river settlement grew the people began a demand for a tribunal located nearer their homes. On Dec. 2, 1771, they clubbed together and agreed to pay "seventy pounds lawful currency" for the erection of a court-house, provided the building be put up in Rockingham. As far as the courts were concerned the king's officers were in full power, and "by extraordinary exertion and by the influence of persons in authority," the court was moved to Westminster. Thus the histories of Rockingham and Westminster were materially changed.

How He
met His
Death.

But the struggle for independence brought on a still more serious complication over the courts. On Sunday, March 12, 1775, a party of Whigs from Rockingham went to Westminster to "dissuade" the Tories from opening court upon the following day. The expedition resulted in the first bloodshed of the American Revolution, and the death of the first martyr, who fell upon what from that day to this has been known as "Court House Hill." As Vermont history records it, the first freeman to fall in the Revolutionary war was William French. He was buried in the Westminster graveyard, where a rough stone records his death thus :

```
      IN MEMORY OF WILLIAM  FRENCH.
     SON TO MR. NATHANIEL FRENCH  WHO
    WAS SHOT AT WESTMINSTER MARCH YE 13TH,
   1775. BY THE HANDS OF CRUEL MINISTEREAL TOOLS.
    OF GEORG YE 3D. IN THE CORTHOUSE AT A 11 A
                   CLOCK
     AT NIGHT IN THE 22D, YEAR OF HIS AGE.
    HERE WILLIAM FRENCH HIS BODY LIES.
    FOR MURDER HIS BLOOD FOR VENGEANCE CRIES.
    KING GEORG THE THIRD  HIS TORY CREW
    THA WITH A BAWL HIS HEAD SHOT THREW.
    FOR LIBERTY AND HIS COUNTRYS GOOD.
    HE LOST HIS LIFE HIS DEAREST BLOOD.
```

The graveyard may be reached by a short drive from Bellows Falls.

In the fight in which French was killed Capt. Joseph Sargeant and his gallant Rockingham militia drove the Tory party from the court-house. In the scrimmage Lieut. Philip Safford was surrounded by the enemy, but succeeded in knocking down ten men

(10)

A LIMITED VIEW OF LUDLOW, LOOKING EAST.

with his bludgeon, and though cut with a sword in the hand of Sheriff Patterson, he retired from the field during the whole *posse* of King George to combat his company.

One Way of Preaching.

When the French and Indians made a raid down the Connecticut valley as far as Deerfield, Mass., early in the eighteenth century, they passed through Rockingham on the return march, and a halt was called there to give the prisoners a chance to rest. While the party was in the town, Rev. John Williams — the famous Deerfield pastor, one of the captives, who became the ancestor of a line of preachers as well as of the Indian branch of the Williams family, through his daughter Eunice, then a captive with him at Rockingham — preached a sermon in order that "all, whether in peace or war, might profit thereby." Rev. Eleazer Williams in later years made a stir by attempting to palm himself off as the last dauphin of France, but he was probably the descendant of Eunice Williams.

A Curious Wedding.

In connection with Rockingham and Westminster comes the story of a curious wedding. In a manuscript letter of Hon. William C. Bradley he says:

By a strange perversion of legal principles during the latter part of the eighteenth century, certain people were led to believe that whoever should marry a widow who was administratrix upon the estate of her deceased husband, and should, through her, come into possession of anything that had been purchased by the deceased husband, would become liable to answer to the goods and estate of his predecessor. The method adopted to avoid this difficulty in the marriage of Asa Averill to the widow of Major Peter Lovejoy was very singular. By the side of a chimney in the widow's house was a recess of considerable size. Across this a blanket was stretched in such a manner as to form a small inclosure. Into this Mrs. Lovejoy passed with her attendants, who completely disrobed her and threw her clothes into the room. She then thrust her hand through a small aperture purposely made in the blanket. The proffered member was clasped by Mr. Averill, and in this position he was married to the nude widow on the other side of the woolen curtain. He then produced a complete assortment of wedding attire, which was slipped into the recess. The new Mrs. Averill soon after appeared ready to receive the congratulations of the company and join in their hearty rustic festivities.

Bellows Falls.

BELLOWS FALLS is the southeastern gateway of Vermont, and every person who by rail enters the confines of the Green Mountain State must, if he comes from the southeast, pass through this historic village. In finding an entrance from Boston the railroad passes at the foot of a mountain of rock so abrupt that with difficulty its crest can be seen from the car windows. On the opposite side, in even closer proximity to the rails, runs the Connecticut; and still farther beyond, the hills rise into mountains overlooking the valley and the river. It was in the gorge at Bellows Falls that Rev. Samuel Peters lodged the

The Southeastern Gateway to the Green Mountains.

most preposterous of his lies about America. He told the good people of England that at Bellows Falls the Connecticut was so swift at flood time that the water, confined "between two shelving mountains of solid rock," became "consolidated by pressure" to such a degree that an iron crowbar could not be forced into it; "there iron, lead, and cork," he added, "have one common weight; and here, sturdy as time and harder than marble, the stream passes, irresistible, if not swift as lightning." Peters was a cheerful liar, but the current is somewhat formidable, and turns many factories that seem almost out of place amid such romantic surroundings.

The trip from Bellows Falls is a continuous excursion even to a business man. There are pastoral scenes, mountain reaches, and bewildering successions of wild landscape that compel the attention of the traveller.

ANOTHER VIEW OF CASTON GORGE, SHOWING A LARGE BOULDER IN THE RIVER

From the valley of the Connecticut to the summit of the Green mountain range the Rutland road climbs to the height of land through passes hewn in solid rock, over bridges spanning brooks and rivers many feet below them, and on the brink of many a cliff and precipice. If the day is dull, clouds hang about the top of the mountains, and as the train emerges from the banks of mist the descent to the valley of the Champlain is made through a wonderful complexity of mountains and lowlands.

As a hamlet Bellows Falls was first known as Fallstown and later as Great Falls. Many years ago it outgrew the village of Rockingham by reason of its water-power. In olden days little stock was taken in the future of the village, and should the venerable Vermont founders arise to-day from their graves, their surprise would be as great as was that of Commander De La Place, of Fort Ticonderoga, when he was awakened in the gray of the morning by the command of Ethan Allen to surrender the fort " in the name of the Great Jehovah and the Continental Congress."

The town has three hotels, the Rockingham, Town's Hotel, and the Commercial House, a number of liveries, good water, and other accommodations usually found in a thrifty Vermont town. The great industry of the village is the pulp and paper mills, where logs are ground and made into paper stock for newspapers. In this line the industry is one of the most extensive in the United States. Sundays excepted, stages leave for Saxton's River, Alstead, Grafton, and Townshend at 12.15 o'clock in the afternoon. Saxton's River is four miles distant, and is the seat of Vermont Academy, a thriving college preparatory school.

Indian Relics, and the Story of Kilburn Mountain. There is evidence that an Indian village was once located in Bellows Falls. The natives were naturally attracted there by the good fishing. For years after the pioneers began to settle about the falls the plowshare brought up many an Indian arrowhead and tomahawk. According to good authority the aborigines buried their dead along the hill where Westminster street now runs. Many years ago where the old "Granger" or "F. B. F." grocery store was erected human bones were found.

Kilburn or Fall mountain, which so boldly marks the entrance to the town, was the scene of a spirited encounter in 1755 between Col. John Kilburn and a large party of Indians. Colonel Kilburn, who was one of the first settlers, built a log hut on the south slope of the mountain. Here with five companions he was besieged by Indians, and running out of lead he is said to have resorted to the clever device of hanging up blankets within the walls, and so catching the spent bullets from the redskins' guns, remoulded them. This is not one of Reverend Peter's yarns and the story is credited by some.

Indian hieroglyphics, cut in a huge rock, appear on the Vermont side of the Connecticut not far below the toll-bridge. It is supposed that these characters were made by Indians upon their triumphal return from the burning of Deerfield, Mass.

Rockingham Village.

WHAT remains of the historic village of Rockingham is little more than a handful of houses nestling in the valley, a stone's throw from the station, where the mail is dropped and where the inhabitants and visitors take and leave the trains.

The village is simply a rustic retreat located in the valley, through which winds the Williams river. If for nothing more it will repay any traveller for his time and trouble to visit the old Congregational church, which, since the year 1787, has seen the devotions of the people of this historic valley. The ancient wooden structure, now sadly out of repair, stands as a primeval sentinel

in the main street of the hamlet, but a short walk from the depot, and is even now occasionally used for worship. Strangely enough, this isolated house of God, with its old-fashioned pews, high pulpit over which is still suspended a sounding-board fastened with hand-wrought nails, has housed not only those bent on godly errands, but rampant politicians as well. For years the church was the only building in the town large enough for political gatherings, and until the "town house" at Bellows Falls was constructed the primitive office-seekers and the good minister divided honors several times in the course of a year.

Bartonsville.

FOUR miles north of Rockingham is the remnant of the town of Bartonsville, named after Jerry Barton, the first settler. In 1869 a flood destroyed the mill-dam, and the hamlet received a financial shock from which it never rallied. There has not been a "house raisin'" in the place for many a day; "corn huskin's" and "parin' bees" are things of the past, and the village may be said to have got its growth.

A Quiet
Village.

Trembling
Chasm at
Brockway's
Mills.

Before reaching Bartonsville there is on the line of the railroad one of the most beautiful spots in Vermont. As the train approaches a point known as "Brockway's Mills" one sees a chasm through which the river runs after falling over a mill-dam. The road crosses the water at a considerable height, and then the south-bound traveller seems bent on piercing the mountain. Suddenly the train turns a sharp curve, sweeps about the base of the mountain, and emerges again into fertile valleys through the lower end of the gorge. The place has been named Trembling Chasm from the seeming vibration of the rocks during high water.

Chester.

ONE can rarely go amiss in selecting a summer resort in the mountain region of the State. Chester, which is in the valley of the Williams river, and not far from Bartonsville, on the Rutland road, is already known to the summer visitor. Many make some preparation for tourists, and nature does the rest.

The drives throughout the surrounding country are a continuous source of pleasure to strangers. Some of the more favorite ones are those through Lovers' Lane to Wyman's Falls, a distance of three miles southeast; through Grafton Gulf, a distance of five miles; Cavendish Gorge, a distance of eight miles north, and Proctorsville Pass, two miles farther on. Windham mountain, ten miles distant, is often the objective point of many a picnic party. The trout-fishing all about the town is good, and in 1898, when two streams, stocked and posted by the State, are opened to the public, there will be no better trouting in Vermont — which is saying a good deal.

It is safe to say that there is not a town in the United States constructed on the plan of this village. It is, in truth, one long street. North of the depot is a small village called North Chester, with a store, a post-office, and a few houses. Next comes Chester Depot, with a post-office, a hotel, and manufacturing interests; and a mile farther on Chester itself, with stores, a post-office, hotel, and a park that would find a favorable setting in a more pretentious town. The three hamlets are as distinct as though they had no

U.S. Mail Train climbing the Mountain.

interests in common, outside of those of a political nature, despite the fact that the street is but three miles in length. Stages run daily, Sundays excepted, to Londonderry, Grafton, Weston, and intermediate points. The Londonderry line touches Simonsville and Lowell lake, and the Weston line passes through the village of Peaseville, in the township of Andover.

Chester is one of the oldest towns in the State and has the distinction of having been chartered three times.

Thrice Chartered. The first charter was granted Feb. 22, 1754, by Gov. Benning Wentworth, of New Hampshire, and was issued to John Baldridge and other pioneers. The town was then known under the name of Flamsted. No settlement was effected, however, at this time, and on Nov. 3, 1761, a second attempt at colonization was made. This time the charter was issued to Daniel Haywood and his associates, and the town was named New Flamsted. A New York charter to Thomas Chandler, Sr., and others was granted July 14, 1766, and the town was successfully organized a year later under the name it bears at the present time. In 1767–68 a court-house and a jail were built by permission of New York. The county was at that time called Cumberland. The jail was a rattletrack affair built of hackmatack logs, and the court-house was not much more thoroughly constructed.

The New York Charter and Acts were made null and void by the struggle over what is called the "Hampshire **Court-House** Grants." But the Vermont towns did not yield without stirring scenes. In addition to the regular run of early **Riots of** incidents in pioneer towns, there is in Chester a bit of history which illustrates some of the characteristics of the **Early Days.** settlers. The inhabitants of Windsor, twelve miles away, for the most part adhered to the jurisdiction of New Hampshire. They denied the authority of the courts established by New York, and resisted the issuing of precepts therefrom. The trouble grew until, in 1770, Col. Nathan Stone, of Windsor, a justice of the peace holding a New York commission, but at heart a coöperator with those who maintained the supremacy of the New Hampshire title, brought matters to a crisis by declaring that no writs or precepts from either of the courts of the county should be served in Windsor. A few days later Sheriff Daniel Whipple and a *posse*, including John Grant, a lawyer, attempted to make arrests in Windsor, but the whole party was captured by Stone and his adherents. On June 4 Stone and a crowd of sympathizers gathered at the Chester court-house, and upset proceedings to such an extent that an adjournment was made necessary. Later in the day John Grant, who, in the words of Stone, was a "bad man," was taken prisoner and marched to Windsor, where, upon his refusal to cease practising in the grants, he was incarcerated for six days.

A traveller cannot cross the Vermont borders without running into bear stories, and he cannot penetrate the **Sunday Bear-** mountain region very far without finding traces of these animals also. There has long been a State bounty on **shooting.** bears killed, but the law is now repealed. Many of these fierce animals are shot or trapped yearly in the forests, and mountaineers who have "ketched an even score o' b'ar" are common enough in southern Vermont. An easy buggy ride from Chester will bring one to the abodes of men who have taken perhaps thirty of them.

There are two kinds of bear stories—the heroic yarn that adorns the literary page, and the real thing. Vermont has both in plenty. There is, however, no excuse for inventing bear stories in the Green Mountain State, for ventures with these black beasts of the forests are commonplaces in her history.

No one who has hunted bears will deny that they are as intelligent as the average man. When a man meets a bear for the first time the bear appears to be the superior animal; that is, he acts the more intelligently, he seems more rational, and even a veteran hunter seems to have a great respect for these animals.

ENTRANCE TO CLARENDON GORGE.

There is not a town through which the Rutland trains run that has not its bear history. Even the half-humorous narratives that have come down from tradition are undoubtedly founded on fact. In a town lying a short distance to the southeast of Chester there is told to this day the exploit of a certain bear and a pioneer, and it is still a question which got the most fame out of it. It seems that a very sagacious bruin lived in a ravine not so very far from a log-house, a corn-field, and a church. This was a dangerous combination for all concerned. The pioneer had a sharp eye, but the bear a sharper one, and it fell out that the latter did most of his feeding in the corn-field when the owner was at church. It finally became a question of corn-crop or the laws of God with the owner of the log-cabin. The corn-crop won. So the pioneer remained at home one Sunday morning, and created a great scandal in the congregation by shooting the bear dead while the good parson was preaching. A special church meeting was called, and the hunter was tried for breaking the Sabbath day. He put forth the stalled-ox-led-to-water argument, but to no purpose. On the following Sunday he sat in his pew armed with his gun, sword, and so on, and when the parson began with the words " Offending brother," the bear-hunter cocked his gun and cried, " Proceed if you dare !" In modern language, he painted that church red, drove out the congregation, locked the church door, sent the key to the parson, and — well, died fourteen years afterward a brother in full communion. Here is a case where an old-time Vermont bear put too much faith in his church-going neighbor. The modern bear does not make that mistake very often, and it takes a shrewd head and a quick eye to get a good crack at one. More bears are trapped than shot nowadays, and yet they are on the increase in many parts of the State.

There are accounts in Vermont towns of announcements from the pulpit of bear-hunts in the days when these animals were the pests of the planters. One good minister by chance was called upon to give notice of a funeral, a wedding, and a bear-hunt on the same Sunday morning, and he was sore distressed to decide which should come first. He selected the bear-hunt, but his reasons, if any, are not known.

One of the most conspicuous landmarks in Chester is the pioneer burying-ground nearly opposite Hotel Fullerton. For over a century and three-quarters this God's acre has received the village dead, and it is to-day covered with curious gravestones. Dates extending back as far as 1716 are found here, as well as epitaphs which those having a touch of the Old Antiquary in them can trace out with no little interest.

To reach Lowell lake, in the township of Londonderry, it is necessary to go either by private conveyance or stage through twelve miles of the foot-hills of the Green Mountain range, along the west branch of the Williams river, to the old village of Simonsville. Before the days of the railroad this hamlet was a post station where well-filled stages from Boston to Manchester, Vt., Troy, N.Y., and Bellows Falls stopped "to bait." The old tavern is now owned by Col. H. O. Peabody and is used for a post-office and store. At the "Summit," where the stage road crosses the foot of Huntley or Globe mountain, is the old Huntley tavern, still in the possession of the Huntley family. In days gone by both these stopping-places did an extensive business.

Lowell Lake.

Lowell lake itself is reached by a road branching from the main stage-line a mile and a half beyond the "Summit." One mile farther on, the irregular sheet of water comes suddenly into view. The lake is a mile long and half as wide, and furnishes excellent bass, pickerel, and pike fishing. Where the road touches the shore is a rustic hotel which, with its cottages, will accommodate seventy-five persons. The hostelry is well kept, and here many guests from Massachusetts and Connecticut make their summer home.

SUMMIT CUT, 1,400 FEET ABOVE TIDE WATER, NEAR THE ENTRANCE TO WHICH WAS UNEARTHED THE
SKELETON OF AN ELEPHANT, DURING THE CONSTRUCTION OF THE RUTLAND RAILROAD.

The locality is not without its history. A short distance from the outlet of the lake is the spot where, in 1777, Gen. John Stark camped for a week while on the march from New Hampshire to Bennington, where he arrived in time to take part in that famous battle on the seventh of August of that year. A short time ago a cannon ball was discovered here. Two more were found about the same time at the upper end of the lake, where, it is said, General Stark and his militia camped for two months while engaged in cutting a road to Manchester, Vt. Two feet under the leaves and woodland *débris* was exhumed a shovelful of charcoal, the remains, probably, of an old camp fire. At the outlet of the lake at a point in front of the hotel is the site where once stood a carding-mill, the machinery for the operation of which was dragged up the mountain on poles hitched to horses.

An Obsolete Burying-Ground. Scarcely a stone's throw from the spot where the carding-mill stood is what is, perhaps, the most obsolete burying-ground in New England. On a small knoll covered with brush and trees of large girth a few battered grave-stones make a brave but unsuccessful attempt to present a half creditable appearance. In the summer cattle and deer roam about these stone sentinels of the dead, and in the fall and winter bears and hedgehogs play among the graves. Though the knoll was partly cleared in the spring of 1896, the larger trees, with their roots firmly imbedded among the bones of the departed settlers, still stand. An explanation as to the origin of this strange cemetery comes from the lips of an old man who says that while General Stark was encamped on the shores of the lake, two soldiers died and were buried there. Later on settlers from Londonderry found the spot a convenient place to bury their dead. The gravestones are similar to those found at Chester and bear the same curious designs cut in blue-gray slabs. The dates run back as far as 1778. A circumstance worthy of note, and characteristic of Vermont graveyards in general, is the old age at which the men and women died.

Fertile Intervales and Abandoned Farms. About the lake are large intervales of rich mountain land where many of the so-called abandoned farms are being bought up and made to pay well. On the "hill road" to Simonsville, Prof. A. K. Marsh, of Harvard University, and his brother, E. D. Marsh, of Boston, have "taken up" several of these farms and are "working" them profitably. Other examples, well suited for the Vermont farmer to follow, are also found about here.

Gassetts.

THE village of Gassetts, a small station between Chester and Cavendish, is in Dutton Gulf, where, in prehistoric times, ran the outlet to the great lake that filled the Black-river valley. The village has many a beautiful drive. The hamlet is visited by persons who begin here a two hours' stage ride to Springfield, Vt., a thriving town in the Connecticut valley. The road to **A Hamlet in a Prehistoric Waterway.** this old New England village strikes the valley of Black river a few miles from Gassetts, and is one of the most beautiful mountain lines in the State. There are wild and rocky woods melting into fertile fields; there are rivers and brooks along the entire course, and the purest wood-scented air to breathe. Hunting and fishing about Gassetts are good, and now and then big game is found. Deer frequent the hills and valleys, and more than one Gassett farmer will tell you that he has repeatedly seen bucks and does feeding in the barn-yard with his cattle.

Some years ago a party from Ludlow heard that a bear was making trouble among the sheep in the vicinity of Gassetts, and half the town, along with the entire dog population, started in pursuit. That night the party returned with the carcass of the bear.

BLACK RIVER VALLEY, LOOKING NORTH. BED OF A PREHISTORIC LAKE.

When asked how they killed the animal a wag in the party declared that the bear was found up a high tree. Upon making the discovery Lawyer ———, of Rutland, well known for his dreary anecdotes, began to tell one of his funny stories, and the animal immediately came down and allowed himself to be killed.

Cavendish.

CAVENDISH, in the valley of Black river, is the first town above Chester, and more than one traveller has been reminded, while exploring its hills and vales, of their resemblance to the intervales of the lower Alps. A small village, but a pistol-shot from the depot, marks the stopping-place of travellers. The hamlet has a busy woollen mill that seems almost foreign to so quiet a community, and a comfortable and neatly appointed hotel on the main street between two long rows of substantial houses.

A Remarkable Spot with an Odd History. The village, which was originally called Duttonsville, was once the bed of a prehistoric lake which extended back four miles to Ludlow. At the lower end of the town Hawks mountain turned the small outlet stream to the right, and the waters flowed to Williams river through Dutton's Gulf, where now lie the tracks of the Rutland railroad. To the left of Hawks mountain a rough valley found its way to the Connecticut near what is now the town of Springfield, Vt. By some subterranean upheaval the outlet of the lake was blocked and its waters were forced to the Connecticut through the valley on the left of Hawks mountain. Slowly the erosive stream wore its way through the gneiss and calciferous mica-schist, eating away, little by little, the softer bowlders, until to-day Cavendish gorge is one of the most wonderful examples of erosion found in the East. Thousands of travellers visit the place each year, and it is often inspected by geologists from all over the United States.

A Bit of Early History. The town received its charter from Benning Wentworth, governor of New Hampshire, under the date of Oct. 10, 1761. Amos Kimball was the principal owner. A year later a number of the proprietors made a survey and allotted shares in severalty. According to their own words they were "great in forwardness when disputes arose," and quarrels over the land titles ensued. The same spirit which dominated the Pilgrims in the struggle for freedom of worship manifested itself in these settlers whenever they had occasion to believe that their rights were trampled upon, and as a result of their quarrels the settling of the town was abandoned until 1769, when in June of that year Capt. John Coffein built a dwelling-house and farm buildings in the northern part of the town on "Twenty Mile Stream Road." A little later other pioneers joined Captain Coffein. To-day the burial-place of these early settlers may be seen. The graveyard is situated in a field close to "Twenty Mile Stream Road."

Strange Birth of the First White Child. Long before Captain Coffein "pitched" at Cavendish, the first white child born in Windham county had put in an appearance in this town. On Aug. 30, 1754, a party of Indians appeared at Number Four, now Charlestown, N.H., and in the gray of morning descended upon the dwelling of James Johnson, who, together with his wife, three children, and several persons living in the vicinity, were taken prisoners. With the rising of the sun the redskins started for Canada, taking their captives with them. The route lay by way of Crown Point. On the evening of the first day the party encamped in the southwest corner of what is now the town of Reading. On the following morning Mrs. Johnson became ill and was carried on a litter. At a point a half mile from the camping-place, and in the present limits of Cavendish, a daughter was born to Mr. and Mrs. Johnson. A rest of a few days was taken, and then the party resumed the journey. The provisions finally gave out and a horse was killed for food. Raw scraps of meat from the animal were given to the infant to suck, and the little one thrived and grew. The child was named "Captive," and in later years, after the family had regained its freedom, the young woman became the wife of Col. George Kimball, of Cavendish.

Near the birthplace stands to-day a rough stone bearing this legend:

This is near the spot that the Indians encamped the night after they took Mr. Johnson and family, and Mr. Larrabee and Farnsworth, Aug. 30, 1754. Mrs. Johnson was delivered of a child a mile up this brook.

When trouble's near the Lord is kind,
He hears the captive cry,
He can subdue the savage mind
And learn it sympathy.

Dutton's Tavern of the Olden Times. One of the old landmarks pointed out to the traveller is the Dutton tavern at the corner of the old Weathersfield turnpike and on the military road from Number Four to Crown Point. In the days of the stage coach Cavendish was a post station, and the stage from Boston stopped daily at the inn. The present road to Chester was once the highway to the Massachusetts metropolis, and wound its way from the tavern across the river and disappeared over the brow of a high hill. To-day this old thoroughfare can be seen from the cars where it is crossed by the Rutland railroad a few rods below the depot. At this point there are imbedded in the banks of the railroad the remains of a cellar wall. When the railroad was built the course of the old highway was changed, and now passes under the tracks a few rods above the old wall.

Four Toots, Four Dinners. When stages began making trips over the mountains from Boston to Rutland and Burlington by way of Cavendish, the Dutton tavern had many visitors. During the latter part of the eighteenth century the stage driver from the south had a novel means of indicating to the "help" at the inn the number of passengers to be present at dinner. As the lumbering vehicle put in an appearance on the brow of the hill the driver would blow as many blasts on a tin horn as there were passengers, and the "help" at the tavern would have a piping hot dinner of meat, vegetables, and a little "trollup" in readiness by the time the coach pulled up at the door.

The distance from Cavendish to Boston by the route taken in those days was computed to be about one hundred and ten miles, and the trip took from two to three days, according to the condition of the roads. The old tavern, with the same latch-string that was hung out to travellers a hundred years ago, is still in the possession of the Dutton family, being owned by the wife of United States Senator Redfield Proctor, a direct descendant of the hospitable proprietor of the inn.

A Venerable Charter. The most interesting document in Cavendish is the charter of the town granted by King George III. through Benning Wentworth. It is deposited in the town clerk's office, where it may be seen. The charter is written on parchment in what is now called the "vertical" hand. The writing is as plain as the spelling is quaint, and has stood the test of one hundred and thirty-five years remarkably well. A ponderous wax seal appended is the most curious adornment of this antique document. After the usual preamble the charter starts out with a sentence long enough to stagger the ordinary reader. It begins thus:

Know ye that we of Our Special Grace, certain Knowledge and Mear motion for the Due Encouragement of Settling a new Plantation within Our Said Province, by and with the Grace of Our Trusty and Well Beloved Benning Wentworth, Esq.; Our Governor and Commander-in-Chief of Our Province in New England and of Our Council of Said Province, have upon Conditions hereinafter made, given and granted; and by these Presents for us Our Heirs and Successors, do give and grant in equal shares unto Our Living Subjects of Our Province of New Hampshire and our other Governments, and their Heirs and Assigns forever, whose names are entered in this Grant, to be divided to and amongst them into 72 Equal Shares, all that tract or parcel of land situate, lying and being within Our Said Province and New Hampshire, containing admeasurement Twenty five hundred acres . . . No more.

The name of the grantees and the boundaries of the land thus granted follow, and then come the conditions upon which the grant is made. Many of these are curious. One sets forth in the most dignified language that a market may be opened one or more days a week; another declares that each grantee must cultivate and plant five acres of land each year, and still another announces that "all white pine and other pine trees fit for masting Our Royal Navy be carefully felled and preserved for use of the King's ships."

The Corn Tax. . A farther condition upon which this land was granted was "that each grantee and their Heirs and Successors" should on each Christmas day for the first ten years give as a tax one ear of Indian corn "if lawfully demanded." From that time on they were to be taxed one shilling for every hundred acres owned.

The charter is duly signed by Benning Wentworth and also bears the signature of Thomas Atkinson, secretary.

Other documents of interest, at least to antiquarians, are the deeds recorded in the early days of the town. The first is dated " March ye 8th, 1781," and conveys land from Jesse Reed to John Coffein.

Celtic Philosophy. From the days of the corn tax comes the story of an Irishman who with a neighbor went to Charlestown to grind a grist of corn. On the way home the Celt's horse showed signs of giving out, and the Irishman, in order to lighten the load and still retain his seat, threw the grain bag over his shoulder, and in full confidence that a hundred weight had been lifted from the animal, bade him " Make tracks for home, and that lively."

Cavendish Gorge. To become fully acquainted with the beauties and mysteries of Cavendish Gorge, it is necessary to procure the assistance of one of the inhabitants, who are always willing and proud to show visitors this freak of nature. However, if one is sure-footed, has a fair bump of locality and plenty of time at his disposal, he can pass a morning very pleasantly alone by the river. The head of the gorge, where erosion first began to be felt, is scarcely a half-mile below the depot, and can be reached by following the railroad to a point on the left marked by the ruins of a stone woollen-mill burned about twenty years ago. A thick grove of hemlock trees beyond a small gate makes a delightful place for lunch, and is the point from whence divers paths radiate to all the principal points of interest. From the head to the foot of the gorge the distance is a quarter of a mile, with the depth from the densely wooded banks to the water varying. Surveys made during the summer of 1896 place the fall at about one hundred feet.

A Prospective Water-Power. Without a doubt this tremendous fall is one of the most powerful water-powers in New England. Plans are already maturing whereby the two-thousand-horse power may be used to generate electricity. This would light the valley of Black river from Ludlow to Cavendish, as well as the town of Chester, and set in motion all the manufacturing machinery in the vicinity.

Brook Trout Caught in Shrewsbury Pond

"EASILY DUPLICATED."

The Head of the Gorge. The waters of Black river begin to feel the suction influence in the meadows above the head of the gorge, and the current quickens perceptibly as the stream approaches the huge bowlders which mark its downfall. A moment later Black river becomes a raging torrent, and is dashed to foam and spray among the rocks. As the course extends, the waters, bent in a mad rush to reach their level, shake the very foundations of the rock-girt banks, until the thundering monotone may be heard far up and down the valley. In high water so swift is the current that a log of large dimensions is borne as an infant in the arms of a giant, and is hurled again and again many feet into the air. From the gneiss rocks that bound the water's path the ever-changing current of the stream is best observed. Here one can cling with safety to some tree and watch from his trembling perch the throbbing flood as it rushes below him.

Lovers' Leap. Every traveller who is accompanied by a resident of Cavendish is shown first of all Lovers' Leap, where the jutting points of mica-schist almost meet near the centre of the river. Even the oldest inhabitant fails to remember any incident connected with the naming of this particular spot, and it is left for each to build a romance that may be a fitting explanation for this cognomen.

Hanging Tree. A little below the leap stands a white birch tree projecting over the water from the edge of the bank. The birch is known as Hanging Tree, from the fact that a person with a head not given to taking erratic turns may, by clinging to it and thrusting his body outward over the cliff, obtain a fine view of the gorge.

Chimney Cave. Still farther down, Chimney Cave, a novel but small subterranean chamber, can be reached by a well-worn foot-path. To enter the cave one must cross a slender plank thrown over a brace of rocks. Once over, one finds himself in a spacious room from which a dark passage leads in the direction from which he has come. By crawling through this and climbing over a bowlder one will see, by looking up, a natural chimney. If the explorer is not too much inclined to corpulency an exit through the shaft will bring him to the Pulpit.

A Pulpit of Nature's Building. One may travel many miles and fail to meet with a more peculiar rock structure than this. Many years ago the waters wore a caldron-shaped basin in a bowlder which now stands on the edge of the high bank. They left the rock in the shape of a pulpit which will hold a dozen persons. From the outer edge a fine view may be obtained, as well as more than one sermon from Nature.

Where Lockwood tumbled. In returning to the head of the gorge the natural course will bring one to Lockwood's Tumble at the lime ledge. Some fifty years ago while one Varnum Lockwood was "getting out" limestone, he fell backwards into the river forty-five feet below. There was little water running, and the old man's companions, thinking him dead, hastened to the spot. To their complete surprise they found the old gentleman standing in the water intently examining his pockets. "I'll be darned if I hain't lost my jack-knife," he exclaimed ; and ever afterward the ledge was known as "Lockwood's Tumble."

CROWN POINT MILITARY ROAD FROM NO. 4 FORT, CHARLESTOWN, N.H., OF THE 18TH CENTURY, — AS SEEN FROM THE CAR WINDOW NEAR CLARENDON.

Baltimore.

THERE is a "town" in Vermont named Baltimore, and it is safe to say that not one New Englander in a thousand ever knew of its existence until the presidential year of 1896 brought it into prominence.

Baltimore is a peculiar and at the same time a notable "town." It is peculiar because there is no "town;" and yet it is probably the smallest town in the world. This paradox is easily explained. Technically speaking, Baltimore is a

A Town that is a Town. "town;" yet should you attempt to find it you would be ready enough to admit that there is none, for you would find no store, no church, no post-office, and, indeed, no hamlet wherein to place them. This seems strange when you come to think that the town has as great a voice in the Vermont House of Representatives as does Rutland with its fifteen thousand inhabitants. But that is Vermont law and must therefore stand unquestioned. It seems still stranger when you find that there are but forty-eight inhabitants and but fifteen of these are voters. Yet all this is a fact, and if you care to pay Baltimore a visit you will find these and many more peculiar things not herein mentioned. Should you decide to go to Baltimore, stop at Cavendish, and, if you can find a guide, engage his services at once; for, while people in Cavendish know pretty much everything, there is hardly a man in the town who will admit ever having visited Baltimore, which is only about eight miles away. So do not be too particular about guides, but start at once over one of the most beautiful roads in Vermont. You pass around the base of Hawks mountain, and before you know it you will be in the "town." If you do not drive through before you discover that you are in Baltimore, you may consider yourself in good luck. When you arrive, you will find that the "town" was originally cut out on a bins containing three thousand square acres, and that the boundaries are unchanged to-day. While the scenery is beautiful, and the fishing and hunting are good, the land is not well adapted for farming purposes on account of the stony soil. Indeed, it is alleged that the farmers' sons are obliged to hold the sheep by the hind legs in order that they may pick the grass from between the rocks. Even bees find it hard to live, and according to Mr. Bryant, the last "town" representative, fifty colonies he once transplanted here died, being unable to subsist on scenery. Baltimore is emphatically a quiet "town," and, if one wishes to leave the cares of the world behind him, he can certainly do so by coming here. There was a wedding in the "town" twenty years ago, and this furnished the universal topic of conversation until ten years later, when a fire occasioned unprecedented excitement. Once there were more citizens there than now, but in one way and another they have disappeared. In the summer the population will reach forty-nine if a veteran now at the soldiers' home in Bennington decides to return with warm weather. This may not exactly cause a boom in real estate, but every addition to the population is welcomed in Baltimore.

It is in a political way that the "town" is most interesting. As there are fifteen voters and seventeen

Why the Town became Notorious. offices to be filled, once a year every freeman is made happy and two doubly so. It is then that in place of a caucus the thirteen Republicans hold what might be termed a swapping bee, and exchange offices for the ensuing year. There are no political bosses and few squabbles, and as a general thing the election which follows the bee is quiet and uneventful. It is right here that Baltimore plunged headlong into notoriety by failing to vote for presidential electors in 1896. In order that an election may be legal in Vermont the list of candidates must be posted at least six days before the election. This was not done. Accounts differ as to the whys and wherefores, but it is a fact that it was considerably less than six days before election when the posters made their appearance. The law also requires the arranging of booths

OTTER CREEK VALLEY, NEAR RUTLAND.
"YES, IT IS BEAUTIFUL."

in compartments as well as the opening of the polls at ten o'clock in the morning in towns like Baltimore. When election day came it was found that nothing had been done in the way of preparation. No polling place had been provided, and, what was still worse, there was not a ballot in the town. About half-past ten o'clock a Baltimore man, who was down at North Springfield, the nearest post-office town, rescued the ballots from the post-office, where they had lain two days, and carried them to Baltimore. They say in North Springfield that a Baltimore official was in that town both these days, but neglected to visit the post-office. When the ballots arrived in Baltimore it was decided that it was too late and that too many formalities had been neglected to warrant the townspeople in casting their votes, and so every one went home. Thus it was that the plurality for the McKinley electors was thirteen less than it might have been had things been otherwise than they were in Baltimore. A few days after the election the official borrowed from the town clerk a copy of the general statutes of Vermont, but he failed to find the clause relating to polling booths. The penalty for neglecting to provide ballot facilities is $500; but the Baltimore officer didn't know that and probably doesn't know it to-day.

Proctorsville.

A SMALL, neat station a mile above Cavendish marks the village of Proctorsville. A large woolen-mill and a cheese factory comprise the principal industries of the village, which is one of the most pleasantly located in Windsor county. Water conducted from Black river through a canal furnishes the power for the factories. In many ways the village is most admirably situated. On two sides the mountains fence in the hamlet, while above and below is the verdant valley of the river,

A Comfortable Village in Black River Valley. dotted here and there with comfortable farm-houses. A drive over the turnpike in either direction is a source of enjoyment to the lover of nature, and a wheeling trip is equally fascinating. If the tourist fancies more pronounced mountain scenery let him take the stage for Amsden, or a private team, and invade the mountain roads. The village is almost a thousand feet above the sea level, and is noted for its bracing air and clear, dry climate. Fishing and shooting are good all about the town, and it is not unusual to see tempting strings of trout brought in.

Ludlow.

L UDLOW lies in the valley of Black river, which runs at the base of mountains so abrupt that the town seems to lie in an immense crater. From the car windows as a train shoots around a long curve from the north the village is seen many feet below, a sea of housetops appearing among the shade trees, while on the bluff beyond Gill Odd Fellows' Home commands a sweep of the valley. In more ways than one the town is a delightful stopping-place. Two hotels on the main

A Town in a Spot where a Lake once lay. street provide for a large number of guests. There are pleasant drives in all directions and an abundance of good fishing in summer. The purest of water and bracing air, added to the other features of the place, give the town an enviable reputation. For tourists bound for the summer resorts as well as others Ludlow is a good town in which to spend a day or more. All passenger trains stop at the station on the heights, and one has the advantage of leaving almost at any time he may choose. Three good livery stables furnish teams to those who may care for a carriage ride. For river scenery one of the best drives is that to Proctorsville and Cavendish, down the old turnpike which was owned by four early settlers who demanded such high toll that the inhabitants revolted and built " shun-pikes," thus flanking the turnpike people. Another drive is that to Tyson Furnace and Plymouth, where the best of trout and other fishing may be found.

The railroad enters Ludlow on its eastern boundary and follows Black river to the village. Then turning north it reaches the pass in the Green mountains two hundred feet above the level of the west branch of the river. The maximum grade at this point is one and a half per cent., or seventy-six feet to the mile. The line of the road near the village lies on the top of an elevation called Hog Back, seventy-five feet in height. Hog Back is forty rods long, and where the old Indian trail followed it, it was, when the road was built, only wide enough to admit of a narrow pathway.

Tyson and the Famous Gold Mines. To reach Tyson and the famous gold mines the way lies through the lake region of Black-river valley, and in the very heart of a country the romantic charm of which is more subtle than that possessed by any other section of the State. Reach Tyson, and you are at a well-known summer resort; but branch from there into the mountains in the gold-bearing region, and you may touch some point where the foot of white man has never trod. In these explored and unexplored recesses in the primeval forest are " pockets " of gold that yet remain to be taken from the ground.

The Road to Tyson. In leaving Ludlow you follow the Plymouth road past two branches marked by bow-legged signboards and continue on to the village of Grahamville. If these wayside indicators, located a mile or two apart, all inform you that Plymouth is ten miles distant, do not be discouraged because Tyson is the half-way stopping-place, for it is but an honest five miles from Ludlow by a road as level as a floor. Leaving Grahamville, the course leads slightly to the east, and passing from the foot of Ludlow mountain skirts the base of a sharp and rugged elevation on the left, and finally follows the shore of Round lake. Here the mountains on either side rise from the water's edge to such a height that their reflections on the surface of the lake confusingly overlap one another. While Round lake is apparently a body unto itself, it is in reality but one of a string of four which are separated by narrow necks forming the main channel of Black river. Like its sisters, the lake twists and turns about the base of the mountains and is dotted with many islands of various sizes and shapes. Leaving the water's edge, before you realize it you are over a hill and soon driving along the shores of Rescue lake, the next in the series, and, finally, a mile and a half farther on, the road reaches Tyson village. The lake has not always been known by the name given, but after the summer cottages began to appear upon the wooded banks, the name was changed as the result of a strange incident. The lake was formerly called Ludlow pond. In August, 1888, a little girl from Cavendish wandered into the woods, and after three days was found on a rock on the east shore of the lake opposite the Silas E. Pinney farm. The child said that one night she had slept in a cave between two small and one large black sheep. The sheep were afterward determined to be a bear and two cubs. Ludlow people believe this story.

At the head of the lake you find Tyson and Tyson Furnace, the Four Corners and the hotel, and other auxiliaries appertaining to this pleasant and well-kept "Kingdom" in the town of Plymouth. There is a store at the hamlet, a church, a graveyard on a hill so steep that no attempt was ever made to draw a hearse up its sides, and so much scenery that it would take one the entire summer to see half of it. There are comfortable houses painted pure white and adorned with scarlet blinds that give so dazzling an effect that one can shut his eyes and almost see a rainbow floating before his vision. There is a brown house in Tyson, and a gray dwelling beside a mud-colored shed, but the prevailing colors are white and scarlet, and he who builds at Tyson invariably follows the fashion and buys red and white paint and no other.

But if you are bound for the mines do not stop at Tyson. Take the road to the right that crosses the neck of **To the Mines.** the lake, follow on past the Scott farm-house, and at the top of a hill you will come to the Four Corners, where there is no signboard to farther indicate your direction. Turn sharply to the *left*, cross a small bridge, and stop at the top of the next elevation. If you are a lover of natural beauty the chances are you will remain here the rest of the day, for from this point there may be seen one of the finest sights in New England. Below you to the left Rescue lake and the great mountains bordering upon it stretch as far as the contour of the land allows the eye to reach, while extending from your feet to the east is Echo lake, and beyond that Adadule, or Amherst lake, disappears in the mountain recesses. From the shores of this body of water rise the twin mountains, the Widow and the Bachelor, so close that their feet almost touch one another. Away to the left stretches Wilderness mountain, hemming in the narrow valley as far as one can see. To cap all, far away in the distance, Killington peak thrusts its rock crest into the clouds at the apex where the two lines of mountains become one.

A half-mile farther on you come to the house of Joseph Allen and leave your horse, for from here to the mines the bridges are unsafe. Opposite the house an old road to the right leads up a hill. Take this and at the top of the first incline you will catch a glimpse of a mountain brook boiling over the rocks at the foot of a deep gorge. Then you will know that you have entered the mysterious gold-bearing belt of Vermont, where money has been lost and found, and where you may try your hand at placer washing. Follow the narrowing path up the mountain side, and with the brook on your right, you pass almost immediately into a rude, wild gorge. Sharp crags rise on either side more than one hundred feet in height, almost shutting out daylight ; stunted trees cling tenaciously to the rocks ; the brook surges at your feet, and in the gloom and stillness, broken only by the monotonous rush of waters, you proceed under the trees toward your destination. A quarter of a mile farther, crossing a rough bridge, and continuing up the noisy stream to another bridge even less securely constructed than the first, you can by glancing to the right see the ruins of a Vermont Eldorado. It was here that thirty years ago placer washing brought to light nuggets of the precious metal. A penstock led from a pond above, and through this the water for gold washing was conducted. The old wooden conduit has long since fallen into decay, but a sharp eye can now and then detect the remains of the wooden trough. Still following the brook, you cross another bridge and come to a small pond where a detour has to be made to the left in order to reach a footbridge over the neck. Crossing the stream on two tottering planks, you continue up the road and suddenly find yourself in a natural amphitheatre in the rocks, and confronted by a few old buildings. On the left rises the most rugged and barren rock-cliff in Vermont ; to the right is a steep hill, and in front, directly behind the buildings, the brook enters from the woods. Here is the home of Henry Fox, the owner of the Tyson gold mines, and you wonder how any human being can content himself in a place so remote and uncanny. Mr. Fox is a bit of the outside world hermitized in this wilderness, and will take time and pains to explain to you the wonders of the subterranean passages and the washings in and about the brook. In summer Mr. Fox lives in the house on the left, but in winter he moves into the building near the brook, as this has a cellar and is the warmer of the two. Step inside and you will find books in plenty, also the instruments and tools of a miner and assayist, and many kinds of minerals on shelf and table. Mr. Fox will, no doubt, be putting the finishing touches to a gold ingot, but he will stop work upon your arrival and offer you his services at once. Mr. Fox is a well-educated Englishman and probably knows as much about minerals and gold-getting as any one in Vermont. He received

his early education in England, and in his younger days visited Denmark, Sweden, and France, and from the latter country went to New York, where he shipped as purser on the "Clyde," "Atlas," and other lines of steamers. After several shipwrecks and many adventures Mr. Fox visited the mines of Venezuela and Central America, and returning to New York became the junior partner in the firm of Richards & Fox, assayists, at 45 Gold street. Finally, ten years ago, he came to Vermont, and becoming interested in the Tyson gold mines he started a stock company. Buildings were erected and operations were begun in the rocky ledge. A horizontal shaft three hundred and sixty feet in length was blasted out of the rock, and a vertical shaft was sunk two hundred and twenty-five feet downward from the crest of the hill to a point where the two meet. Though the gold-bearing vein was only reached when operations were suspended, the $100,000 and more expended was taken out in gold and $75,000 in dividends were paid. Before the main stratum was reached it was voted to buy new machinery, and the old plant was sold to the Lincoln Iron Works in Rutland. The stock was non-assessable, and the stockholders, contented as long as the metal came into their pockets, would not submit to assessments, and the mine finally became the property of Mr. Fox. One thing is certain: there is gold in those diggings. The question is, Will it pay to get it out? Mr. Fox argues that if ingots of gold were obtained in reaching the main stratum it will certainly pay to mine the auriferous ledge that is now exposed. So great is his confidence that there is untold wealth hidden in the rocks, that he recently refused $25,000 for the mine.

The Rock Mine. Leaving his work, Mr. Fox will take a lantern and conduct you to a building a stone's throw from his house at the base of the rock ledge, and after bolts have been withdrawn and a padlock unsprung you will find yourself at the opening of the famous Rock mine. At one side of the bare room is a dark aperture, some six feet broad by eight feet high, with a car track at the bottom, and you rightly guess that here is where the gold of years ago was taken out. Entering this opening with the uncertain light glimmering in the distance, you follow through this passage in the solid rock for a number of rods. Here a halt is made, and by the aid of the lantern you will see anywhere on the rock shining particles of gold. Some are as fine as a pin-point, while others as broad as your finger-nail stud the quartz. Still further traces of gold will be seen, and as you continue through the moist and dripping passage the wealth of Aladdin appears on every hand. At the end you can see the entrance of the vertical shaft and the main gold-bearing quartz that has yet to be worked. Mr. Fox is authority for the statement that all along the passage the gold assays at $600 to the ton and reaches a greater percentage at the terminus. Returning through this continuous sparkling vault once more into the open air, Mr. Fox will return with you to his house and no doubt show you nuggets of gold that he has rescued from the brook and from the rocks. In another room are specimens of minerals that Mr. Fox has found during his prospecting trips in and about Tyson. A mineralogist could spend a week's time here with profit. The cabinet of specimens includes magnetic iron, magnesia iron, black oxide of iron, arsenic pyrites, fine specimens of agate, garnets an inch in diameter, blocks of amethyst, emery sapphires, galena soapstone, tale crystals, asbestos fibres a foot and a half in length, quartz, black jasper, and black magnetic sand. All these minerals Mr. Fox has found.

Gold Brook. Gold brook, near which the mine is located, rises in Reading pond near the Plymouth town-line and empties into the Black-river lakes. Along its entire course gold has been taken by placer miners, and that there is more there no one gainsays. Operations began fifty years ago and have continued at broken intervals ever since. A branch of Gold brook, known as Buffalo brook, rises in a spring at "Slack's School-house" and finds its outlet a quarter of a mile above the Rock mine. Four miles north is Fife Corners, where thousands of dollars' worth of gold were taken

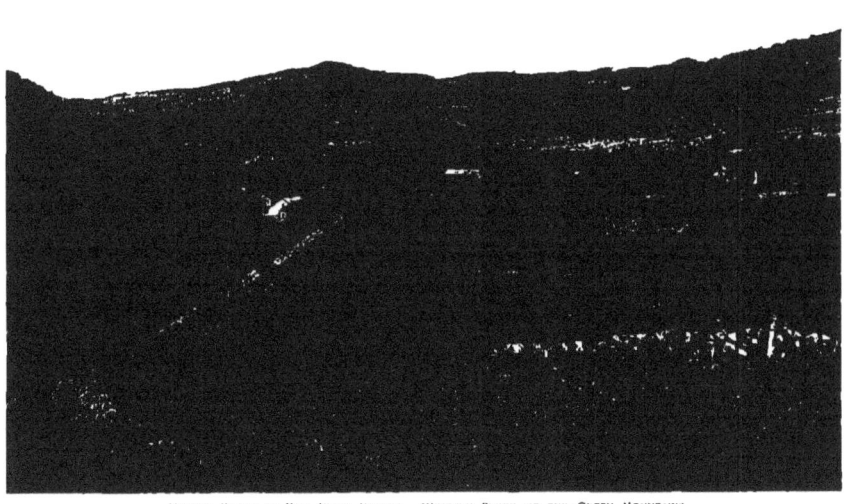

UPLAND FARMS IN MILL RIVER VALLEY. WESTERN SLOPE OF THE GREEN MOUNTAINS.

a few years ago by placer mining. Trout swarm in the streams over the gold beds, and there are few places in the State where fishing is better in public waters. It is even said that the trout are yellow-bellied from so long swimming over the metal.

Mr. Fox has named his house "Gold Brook Chateau," and here he lives alone the year round, seldom going farther than Tyson, for his mail and provisions. At the very mouth of the mine Mr. Fox spends his days and nights without so much as a cat to keep him company.

Gold Brook Chateau.

Healdville.

ONE thousand four hundred and thirty feet above tide-water lies the quaint village of Healdville, the very centre of what in Vermont the woodsmen call the trapping belt. From its height upon the mountains comes that dry climate which with pure air and water makes the inhabitants in this vicinity remarkable for their longevity. From early fall until late in the spring the village is the headquarters of the hardy trappers who follow this trade and "say nothin'" the season through. Each has a particular run, and woe be unto the fellow-trapper who sets his snares upon another's territory. The woods in the vicinity of the village are full of small game, and now and then a bear or lynx is caught. The trappers do not always tell where they got their game unless perchance you are a remarkably good shot, or some particular friend of some particular friend of theirs. A good eye and a steady nerve in manipulating a rifle go a good way with these shrewd men of the woods, with whom it is well to be on good terms if you are spending a season in the mountains, for all woodsmen are profound admirers of a good shot.

The Centre of the Trapping Belt.

In the summer of 1896 one of these trappers boarded a south-bound train at Healdville. He had in two boxes in the baggage-car seven lynx skins, sixty-three fox pelts, thirty-two skunk skins, a hundred odd muskrat hides, and a few mink skins. He "an' another feller had," he explained, "ketched 'em" that fall, and he was taking the lot to the Boston market. The trapper was one of the best known in the State, and a man who spends his life in the Green mountains hunting and trapping in the fall and winter, fishing in the spring and early summer, and looking for gold the remainder of the year. He once had a peculiar adventure with a bear and was urged to tell it. His story ran thus:

"'Twas this way: One mornin' last winter me and Middle Jim, that's my partner, me an' Jim heard tell of a baar in the cuts above Healdville. And I says to Jim, 'Let's git him.' Jim he was 'greeable enough, but a catermounut ez he hed ketched in a trap the week before havin' dug into his shoulder some, and that bein' painful, he wanted to put it off a day, sayin' ez the baar was arter honey an' would stay 'round. So I started out on my run o' traps, and thinkin' ez I'd surprise Jim I moggied along the line arter the baar. A light snow hed fallen the night afore, an' I found the tracks crossin' the railroad a mile above the depot jest where Site Pettingill hed said they were. The tracks went plumb inter the woods on the south side where a big white birch leans toward the track, and then went aroun' a hill and outer sight. I follered along fer half a mile au' all uf a suddent I kum smack up agin a tree with a hole at the bottom two fut across. There the tracks stopped — an' likewise me. I kinder kalkerlated thet the baar was up in the inwards uf thet tree a suckin' honey. An' sure enough he was, fer by lookin' up the hole I c'uld see his hind laigs. He seemed in no partic'lar hurry to kum down, so I give him a jab with the eend uf my gun. On that he climb up further. Then I got some dry leaves and teckled his tail with a leetle smoke and

A Trapper Tells a Bear Story.

CITY OF RUTLAND, SHELTERED BY THE GREEN MOUNTAIN RANGE.

fire. That fotched him, and when he came out I was the most surprised man in the caounty, for that bar was covered with honey from head to fut. I fired and the creetur dropped. He laid so still that I thought he was dead, and goin' up I tuck holt o' him. But I had no sooner tetched him then the darned rascal grabbed me and tried on his leetle huggin' game. He was worse an' a gal Jim uster spark down tu Ludlow, and before I knew it we was both rollin' around in the snow and leaves. By an' by I got out my knife and fixed the bar. Then I took a look at myself, an', say, take honey, an' leaves, an' sticks, an' I'll be blamed ef you c'uld tell which was the bar and which was me. 'Twas no use tryin' to clean up, so I skun the bar and put for home. I surprised Jim."

This hunter is but one of the many who spend considerable time in the summer prospecting for gold. If they are secretive as to where they find game they are clam-like when the gold subject is touched upon. It is well known that there are "pockets" of the precious metal hidden about the mountain brooks, and it is not uncommon for woodsmen to bring in for sale lumps of "color quartz." Just where they get it is one of the secrets of the trade.

Before reaching Bellows Falls the hunter of bear and honey fame grew more confidential and drew from a chamois-skin bag two pieces of ore which, he said, would assay at $1,000 to the ton. Where he got it is a mystery to all but the hunter.

The Summit.

Above the Clouds. SHOU'LD you pass the Summit on one of the fast trains you will catch a glimpse of a bit of a station and a comfortable farm-house, and suddenly feeling an increase of speed you will shoot into the woods and out into an open but rocky and unsettled country. If you come from the north there will be a rush and a roar as the train plunges into the great cuts beyond the depot. These are from forty to seventy-five feet in height and three-quarters of a mile long. With its altitude of one thousand five hundred and twenty-seven feet above the Atlantic, this wild spot is one of the most romantic in the country. It is the height of land on the Rutland road, the watershed of the Green-mountain range, and a point from whence the land on the east slopes to the Connecticut and on the west to the Champlain. When not in the clouds the peaks surrounding the spot where the road crosses stand out in the rarefied air and become a vivid green in winter as well as in summer. The Indian trail from the Connecticut valley to Canada passed where the depot now stands, and the spot was a meeting place for parties going from the Otter to the Connecticut and from the Connecticut to the Otter. The camping ground was at a point just opposite the site of the present depot. Here was a famous cold spring and a clearing just open enough to suit the taste of the natives. The spring is there to-day, and if one chances to look out as the train stops for the conductor to register he will see the train men fill the water jar there.

The Summit is an important point on the railroad, for it is where "double headers" become "single headers" after hauling freight trains up the mountain sides.

As it was in days gone by, so the Summit is to-day a Mecca for sportsmen and fishermen. A deer-runway extends along the ridge of land from the mountains in the southern part of the State to the "yards" on Killington, Pico, and Shrewsbury, and deer are not infrequently seen about here. It was not so many years ago that the passengers on a fast express over the Rutland road were startled when the train was brought to a sudden stop in the cuts. The locomotive had struck and killed a bewildered deer.

A Deer trees a Game Warden. In the fall of 1895, while a game warden from the southern part of the State and a friend from the same section were hunting foxes a mile north of the Summit, a full-grown buck, disturbed by the baying of the hound, dashed into the clearing where the hunters stood. The animal was frightened and ugly, and stood a picture of defiance. The warden laid down his gun and approached the deer. When within five rods of the animal the buck lowered his antlered head and uttering a peculiar low moaning sound started for the warden, who lost no time in climbing the nearest tree. There he stayed for over an hour before his companion could sufficiently and safely attract the animal's attention to allow the warden to descend from his undignified position.

Fishermen find the Summit a convenient place at which to stop, for from this point a short walk will bring one to the head-waters of Mill river or the brooks that flow eastward into the tributaries of the Connecticut. The fishing is excellent, and one may cast a fly down brooks on either side of the mountain to one of the small stations, where he can take an evening train for home.

The inhabitants of the Summit have a reason which they give for the few homes in the community. They declare that the land is so steep on either side of the ridge that everything not nicely adjusted rolls off. Water began first and took with it the rocks along the streams. Then came a general exodus of horses, cattle, yellow-legged pullets, pole-cats, and other adjuncts to civilization, and finally a few of the inhabitants.

Finding of a Remarkable Skeleton. When the contractors began to clear the rocks in the vicinity of the Summit preparatory to blasting, they were obliged to clean out a pond or pot hole not far from where the station now stands. After the water had been removed the men found a bed of mud, and in the mud the skeleton of a huge elephant. The bones were taken out and sent to Boston, where they were put on exhibition in the Museum of Natural History.

In connection with the building of the railroad was one of the most remarkable accidents recorded in history. The facts are presented for this book by Dr. Edward H. Williams, of the Baldwin Locomotive Works. Dr. Williams says :

Having graduated in medicine in 1847, I commenced practising in a little village called Proctorsville, in the township of Cavendish, Vt. The Rutland and Burlington railway was then in process of construction through the town, and as surgeon I attended any of the workmen injured in the vicinity of my residence, including Ludlow and Mount Holly. East and south of me, where heavy work was going on, Dr. James M. Harlow, residing in the village of Duttonsville (now Cavendish), performed similar services.

About six o'clock on the evening of the 15th of September, 1848 (I think that was the day of the month), a man came and requested me to go to Duttonsville and treat one of the foremen, Phineas Gage, who was injured by a blast which occurred some half-hour or more previous. He said that Gage's skull was fractured, and that he was otherwise injured. On the representation that Dr. Harlow was temporarily absent and that my presence was required, I went immediately to Duttonsville. I found the injured man sitting on the veranda of the village hotel coolly talking to those who were gathered about him. I noticed immediately that his skull was fractured, and could see the pulsation of the arteries of the brain. I noticed, also, small portions of the brain escaping from the wound, with a small quantity of blood. On further examination I noticed a slit, two inches or thereabouts in length, on the lower part of his left cheek at the angle of the jaw. I was told that the workmen were charging a blast, and having put in the required quantity of powder, and upon that a small quantity of sand, Gage struck the tamping-bar into the hole to ram down the charge, when an explosion took place, the bar penetrating and passing through this opening in the cheek and coming out on the top of the head, at the junction of the sutures, about where the soft spot is usually on an infant's head. One of the men said the bar went about fifty feet into the air and fell in the road, and was then lying there all covered with blood and brains. The blow knocked the man over, but after a moment or two he sat up and told the men to quit work, and asked if Ben Warren, the man who furnished coal to the different smiths' shops along the line, had not just passed, and if so to keep him and he would ride home with him. The cart was brought back and Gage walked to it, getting in and sitting up. I suggested then that a room be got ready in the house for the patient, and he, unassisted, walked upstairs, and after undressing him we put him to bed in a large dance-hall connected with the house, where there would be plenty of light and air. I then examined him more thoroughly and found that the skull had been fractured in a circle some three inches, at least, from the centre of the wound, particularly on the sides and back around the wound, so that

[41]

the whole top of the head was pushed up like a funnel. The optic nerve of the left eye had been cut off in the passage of the bar, and the cheek-bone had been pushed out an inch or more from its position. During all this time blood was running down his throat into his stomach. This he would occasionally vomit up, together with the food he had eaten at dinner. Dr. Harlow having arrived, we shaved the injured man's head, put on compresses and bandages, and remained with him (at least I did) until about eleven o'clock at night. He gradually grew weaker, but remained conscious, speaking to the various foremen and others who came into the room, even calling them by their names as soon as he heard their voices. His recovery occupied at least three months, during which time he suffered no pain, and there was no inflammation from the wound. His mind was clear from the time of the accident until his ultimate recovery.

I would add that I knew Gage well before he met with the injury, as I was a frequent visitor to the pit where he was employed, being interested in the curious formation of the rock that existed there, and I noticed he was a bright, active young man, twenty-five years of age, steady and accustomed to heavy work, and had been employed during the construction of the Hudson River railway, and was often a witness to severe accidents. From the first he made very light of his injury, and frequently told me that he would recover and be as well as ever he was. After his recovery he was about the town, and I took him to the medical college at Woodstock, Vt., with the tamping-bar, in order that the professors and students might see him. The bar was an inch and a quarter round, iron, three feet six inches long, and tapered at the upper end down a distance of eight inches to half an inch in diameter at the lower end.

I would supplement this narrative by saying that Gage went to Chili, and after his recovery was employed on public works there, dying at Santiago de Cuba about the year 1869. He expressed a desire that after his death Dr. Harlow should have his skull as well as the bar, and the two are now in the Museum of the Massachusetts Medical College in Boston.

SANTA BARBARA, CAL., Jan. 6, 1867.

Edward H. Williams.

Mount Holly.

A Picturesque Hamlet once known as "Jackson's Gore."

THE town of Mount Holly, three miles below the Summit, is on the western side of the mountain range. Away to the west lies the broad valley of the Otter, with the stream gliding between the distant mountains on its way to join the Champlain. On one side are the summits of Killington, Pico, and Shrewsbury, and on the other the marble range lying west of Rutland and the Clarendons. Clad in green throughout the entire year, these mountains never fail to rest the eye. Fishing in the trout streams that run down the hillsides is more than ordinarily good, and fair fish may be taken in Mill river. Vast tracts of woodland beyond cultivated fields make the best of cover for small game, and grouse, fox, and hare hunting bring good results. There are not as many foxes now as before the sixty-cent State bounty law set half the idle men and boys to thieving the burroughs, but the sport is still pursued with good success. Occasionally a bear is seen, but bruin hangs pretty closely to the heights of land.

Josiah and the Bear.

Not so many moons ago a farmer named Josiah Bugbee caught sight of a bear in a tree in the apple orchard in the rear of his barn. Arming himself with a rifle and taking with him Blunder, a mongrel hound pup, Josiah set forth. Follow the highway to a point one mile below the Summit, marked by the junction of a rail and barbed-wire fence, turn to the southwest, and at the end of a hundred rods you will reach a hollow stump about twenty feet high. This is where Josiah, the pup, and the bear brought up late that afternoon. Blunder reached the spot five minutes before his master, and when Josiah arrived he was howling at the foot of the stump. At the base of this stump was a hole, on one side two feet across, and directly opposite was an aperture four inches in diameter. Josiah stripped off his coat, divested himself of his coonskin cap, and thrust his head and shoulders into the larger of the holes. Blunder, frantic with excitement, posted himself

Seven-Pound Brook Trout
Taken with a Fly in Shrewsbury Pond.

"AS GOOD FISH REMAIN," ETC.

opposite the smaller aperture. Suddenly a tuft of black hair protruded from the hole, and in a flash Blunder had seized it, and setting his fore-feet against the stump pulled with might and main. With the first jerk came a succession of wild, muffled howls from within the stump, and a moment later Josiah appeared with both hands covering the top of his scalp, from which a considerable portion of the hair was missing. That was a sad day for Blunder, and when he and his master reached home that night it was with a different kind of a *bare* skin from that after which the two so cheerfully set out earlier in the day.

Mount Holly was not an original township, for in surveying the grants on the east and west sides of the range there was left between Ludlow on the east and Wallingford on the southwest a parcel of land called " Jackson's Gore," from Abraham Jackson, an early settler. In 1792 the gore was incorporated as Mount Holly by adding to it all the land between the gore and the Ludlow line. Prior to this, in 1786, settlers located three miles east of the Jackson farm. Strange to say, neither the people at the gore nor the east-siders knew of the existence of the other settlement, and it was only by a strange accident that the pioneers became acquainted.

A Dog barked and What came of it. One Sunday morning a number of the settlers on the east side started out in search of lost cattle, and after travelling west for an hour, they were surprised to hear the barking of a dog. Following the sound, they soon came to Ichabod G. Clark's log cabin, which stood forty rods northwest of the present railroad depot. At the cabin the people of the gore were assembled for religious worship, and thus the two little communities became acquainted.

East Wallingford.

EAST WALLINGFORD, in the heart of the woodcock grounds, is three miles from Mount Holly and thirteen miles from Rutland. From the nature of the soil flights of woodcock stop about here to feed while on their nocturnal journeys south in the fall of the year, and dogs and guns are successfully brought into play during the warm September and early October days. The grounds are small patches of moist woodland lying not far distant from the railroad and within easy walking distance of it. While the scenery lacks the boldness which characterizes the towns lying farther up the mountain sides, it has a peculiar charm. From the railroad tracks a magnificent view of the valley of Mill river may be obtained. The stream lies at a considerable distance below the road, until it becomes almost a gorge along which the line winds. A short distance from Wallingford proper are White Rocks, a cliff of quartz that can be seen for miles down the valley of Otter creek. The famous ice beds about White Rocks are named from the fact that in the hottest days in summer ice can be found in them. The spot is a great favorite with Rutland people, and there is scarcely a week in the summer when one does not find parties picnicing here.

In the Heart of the Woodcock Grounds.

At Northam, a few miles back in the mountains from East Wallingford, one may enjoy good trouting in any of the streams.

On the last day of August, 1896, three men from Rutland fished from six o'clock in the morning until three o'clock in the afternoon with what scarcely might be called meagre luck. The day was hot and a long-continued "dry spell" accounted for the poor fishing. At three o'clock the fish began to bite, and at four o'clock each fisherman had filled a ten-pound basket with plump trout. Fifteen minutes past four a heavy storm, the first in days, put an end to the sport.

A STUDY IN REFLECTION.

[REVERSE THE PICTURE.]

Cuttingsville.

CUTTINGSVILLE, ten miles east of Rutland, is something of a rendezvous for fishermen. From here Shrewsbury lake and many streams may be reached. It is not uncommon on any summer day for a party of sportsmen to board an evening train at this point with baskets of trout that will almost make one forget to hand out his ticket. Cuttingsville is a well-conditioned hamlet in a narrow valley, and is a favorite with many people who spend the hot season at the hotel and farm-houses about the town. It is a pleasant drive from Rutland, and in winter is noted for its New Year's ball, which is attended by people for miles around. The town is the stage station for Shrewsbury, North Shrewsbury, and Cold River. At any of these places will be found the finest of trouting. At Cold River, about "Burditt's Mills," large numbers of trout may be taken from the branches of Cold river. The country is especially wild, and it naturally follows that hunting is good. A half-dozen Canadian lynxes were captured about the "Mills" during the fall of 1896, as well as foxes, grouse, and squirrels without number. The territory is so far back from civilization that it is little hunted and fine sport is thus afforded.

Shrewsbury Lake. Two miles from Cuttingsville lies one of the most famous trout lakes in the State. In the colloquial dictionary it figures as "Sewsbury pon'; " by fishermen it is called Lake Shrewsbury or Shrewsbury Lake. To reach this body of water from Cuttingsville one drives to the northern edge of the village on the road to Rutland and takes a turn to the left leading up a hill. A mile and more of steep climbing brings one to "Phillipses," where a horse may be put up, and where one can leave twenty-five cents for the use of a boat. Anybody at "Phillipses" will show you the pasture path that runs northward for a quarter of a mile and ends at the lake. As you reach the top of the last elevation you see lying before you an oblong and regular sheet of water of considerable size, and so deep that in many places a sixty-foot line will scarcely reach the trout bed. On the shore near where you will prepare to wet your leader is a small building dropped among the trees. This is the shooting box of a number of Rutland sportsmen organized under the name of the Shrewsbury Fishing Club. The lake is public water and is justly famous for its large brook trout, there being none of the lake variety caught here. The water comes entirely from springs on the lake bed and about the densely wooded banks, which, by the way, abound in squirrels, grouse, and deer. Situated as it is in a hollow on the top of a high hill, the nights are cool and a heavy blanket is found to be of service by those who pitch a tent.

During the summer of 1896 the members of the club spent considerable time at the lake and caught some of the handsomest strings of trout ever taken into Rutland. One catch is shown in an accompanying illustration. One beauty captured on a five-ounce rod by E. White, of Rutland, weighed two pounds and three-quarters. The fish was struck not many rods from the shore and took a bait. Fly-fishing is made impracticable in some parts of the lake, as the water is so deep that the trout, lying on the beds, fail to be attracted by the feather. A white miller for evening fishing, and coachman-brown hackle and scarlet ibis for afternoon sport, are the favorite flies. On account of the altitude there is a sameness of atmospheric conditions throughout the summer, and a few standard flies will suffice for a season's fishing. During times of extreme humidity the trout will take grasshoppers.

Two Bushels of Trout. The lake has long been known as a place where fine fish could be taken. As far back as the time of Ethan Allen the lake was often visited by pioneers. As late as 1866 two men with a seine took two bushel-baskets of trout in two hauls.

ONE OF THE MANY MARBLE QUARRIES NEAR RUTLAND.

The hunting for small game is exceptionally fine, and is growing better each year. In the fall of 1896 three men from Rutland shot in one day twelve black ducks, five grouse, a number of gray squirrels, and a marauding hedgehog.

The Clarendons.

CLARENDON means more than the name would naturally imply, for embraced in the township are several small villages, two of which only are reached by the Rutland road. These are East and North Clarendon. As the line of the road descends toward Otter-creek valley the intervales broaden into rich and fertile fields interrupted only by Clarendon Gorge, the most picturesque spot in the township. Through this gorge Mill river fairly boils on its way to the Otter, and has long since cut a deep path through the solid rock. The gorge is visited during the summer by many picnicers, who find here a most enjoyable place to spend a day.

The Home of Judge Theophilus Herrinton. Most of the settlers of the Clarendons came from Rhode Island, and many descendants of the old pioneer families are still found in the valley. The settlers held their lands under a lease obtained of Col. John Henry Lydius, an Indian trader, who was the first title claimant. Lydius claimed to have purchased from the Mohawk Indians, in 1732, a tract of land which, he said, extended sixty miles southward from the mouth of Otter creek, and was twenty-five miles in width. The settlers were obliged by agreement to pay the trader one ear of Indian corn each year for the first twenty years, and five shillings a year after that, for each hundred acres of land rented by them.

At one time the inhabitants living on the road now running between Rutland and North Clarendon became involved in a dispute with other land claimants, and the Lydius deed proving worthless, the original occupants procured a grant under the governor of New York, although it was well known that King George had, in 1767, forbidden the issuing of such a document. One Jacob Marsh bought land under this grant and was among the foremost in advocating the New York and discrediting the New Hampshire title. Marsh was ably seconded in this by Benjamin Spencer, who was said by Ira Allen to be an "artful, intriguing, and designing man." Marsh and Spencer raised the ire of Ethan Allen and his band of Green Mountain Boys, and one Saturday night they appeared in front of Spencer's house, which was not far south of where the H. H. Dyer farm is now located. Allen, Remember Baker, and other well-known actors of that day, entered the house about eleven o'clock, and taking Spencer into custody, marched him two miles through the woods to the house of one Green, where he was kept under guard until Monday morning. He was then taken to the house of Joseph Smith and a trial was ordered. Spencer requested that this take place in front of his own door, and the request was granted. In front of Spencer's house a "judgment seat" was erected, and upon this Allen, Baker, Seth Warner, and Robert Cochran took their places as judges. Spencer was charged and convicted with "cuddling with the land jobbers of New York" and many other like offences. As a penalty it was announced that Spencer's house and goods should be burned, but the convicted man begged so hard that finally the sentence was revoked and the house was deroofed. The sentence was executed "with great shouting and much noise and tumult." Marsh, who was in New York at the time, was caught upon his return and given such a liberal application of the "beech seal" that his back stung for many a day under the chastisement he received with the "twigs of the wilderness."

"A Bill of Sale from God Almighty." A Clarendon character was the far-famed Judge Theophilus Herrinton, or Harrington, as the name is commonly but incorrectly spelled, who refused to deliver a runaway slave to his master without "a bill of sale from God Almighty." Judge Herrinton came to Clarendon from Rhode Island in 1785. He married in his former home Betsey Buck, and in 1797 there were living eleven of their twelve children. The longevity which characterizes Vermonters is brought to mind in this connection, as there were at this time in one school district in Clarendon eight families to whom had been born one hundred and thirteen children, of whom ninety-nine were then living. None of the husbands in these families had a second wife.

Judge Herrinton represented Clarendon in the Legislature in 1795 and from 1798 to 1803 inclusive, and was speaker of the House of Representatives in the last-named year. He was chief judge of Rutland County Court from 1800 to 1803, when he was elected judge of the Supreme Court, in which capacity he served for ten years.

Of Judge Herrinton Hiram A. Huse says: "He was no observer of conventionalities, if he knew them, and it has been said that he sometimes went into court barefooted. His business was that of a farmer, and he was not admitted to the bar till after his election as a Supreme Court judge. Many stories are told of him — how he said he didn't know as the court knows what a demurrer is, but it knows what justice is, and the plaintiff shall have judgment; and how, while the other judges doubted whether the horse thief who stole in Canada, and was guilty of asportation in this State, could be here convicted, Herrinton insisted that he not only stole it in Canada, but every step of the way he took with it, and so stole it all the way through Vermont; and how he cut the knot about the seal by his 'Hand me a wafer.'"

Rutland.

IN a valley in the very heart of the Green-mountain range, yet in direct communication with the principal cities of the country, lies Rutland, one of the most important municipalities in northern New England. It is, moreover, a city combining the advantages of a metropolis and the beauties of a country town; a city of homes and a centre of culture and refinement. Its altitude of five hundred and sixty-two feet above the level of the sea gives it a bracing air, and its water for the carafe

A City of Marble in the Heart of the Green Mountains. and the extinguishing of fire, coming as it does from ice-cold springs far back in the mountains, is of a purity unquestioned. A jar of water taken a few years ago from a city hydrant was sent to a Boston laboratory for analysis, and the reply came back that but one jar had ever been received the contents of which had shown upon test to be purer than the Rutland water. The same is used now as then, although the rapid growth of the city has made it necessary to increase the capacity of the settling ponds.

This particular part of the valley of the Otter has a much more even temperature than might be thought by a stranger who associates Vermont with all the bad weather and cold storms charged up against the account of New England. Rutland lies just out of the track of the greatest storms. The marble range on the west, and Killington, Pico, Shrewsbury, East mountain, Hall mountain, and other peaks of the Green-mountain range to the east, stand as buffers between Rutland and the storms which the clerk of the weather bureau gets up against the peace of this community. As a rule the most severe storms break on one side or the other of the city, which thus reigns in a happy valley which has long attracted the attention of the traveller. The balsam and spruce covered mountains send down cooling breezes in summer and temper the sharp winds and produce a notably even climate for this latitude.

As a business centre Rutland is unquestionably the first in the State. Its many machine-shops and wood-working industries give employment to hundreds of men who are rapidly acquiring homes in the city. The stores and hotel accommodations are especially good. There are several hostelries " close handy by " to the railroad station, and still others may be found farther out. Among the nearer hotels are the Berwick, Bardwell, Brunswick, and Banquet. One minute's walk from the electric-car line will bring one to the Brock House, which is run more on the boarding-house plan than as a transients' hotel. The residence of the late Ex-Governor John B. Page has been thrown open to guests, and is a notably good place in which to spend the summer.

Rutland is the railroad centre of the State, and is on the direct line between Boston, Montreal, Ottawa, and the West. Take a train at Boston at 11 o'clock in the morning, and at 4.40 o'clock in the afternoon you will find yourself in the Rutland station in time for a drive to any of the lake or mountain summer-resorts before taking a 6-o'clock dinner. Take your rod and fly book with you; wet a line after your dinner and again in the morning; drive to Rutland in time to catch the Green-mountain Flyer for Boston at 1.55 o'clock in the afternoon, and you will be at the " Hub " at 7.35 o'clock that evening.

The city of Rutland, like its surrounding country, impresses the traveller with its beauty. The streets are broad, the houses well built, and in many cases handsomely planned, and comforts found in a much larger municipality may be had at a nominal cost. The only State institution in the city is the House of Correction, which is situated on a commanding hill overlooking the church spires.

Pleasant Drives to Pleasant Places. A drive from Rutland in any direction is a treat within the reach of almost any pocket-book, for a good horse and comfortable carriage can be had for from $2 to $3 for the day. If you go to the north you follow the winding course of the Otter to the famous falls of Proctor or the town of Pittsford; drive to the south and your course lies through the same verdant valley to the White Rocks at Wallingford, or the mysteries of the gorge at Clarendon; go to the west and you will see the renowned quarries of marble at West Rutland, or enter the lake region of Castleton and Poultney; drive east and you will pass over the summit of the Green-mountain range, where houses are few and far between, but where bears, deer, and lynx are no strangers. Any of the points mentioned are within an easy drive from the city over the best of mountain and valley roads.

Killington Peak. Ask a Rutlander to tell you the point of most general interest in this vicinity, and if it is a summer day he will reply without hesitation that it is Killington peak. Four thousand two hundred and forty-one feet above the sea level, this peak stands the king of Vermont mountains. From the United States Signal Service pole, on the highest point of vantage, one can see with the naked eye from the Canadian border on the north to the Massachusetts line on the south, and from the White mountains beyond the Connecticut on the east to the Adirondacks beyond the Champlain on the west. With an ordinary telescope Burlington can be seen on any clear day. A few years ago, when a party of engineers connected with the United States Coast Survey were stationed on the mountains, a large telescope was levelled on New York harbor, and a flash of light reflected from a mirror held by preconcerted arrangement in the statue of Liberty was plainly observed.

To reach the peak by the most direct route one leaves Rutland by way of Killington avenue, and is driven to the top of the

BEAUTIFUL LAKE HORTONIA.

"Notch," to a point from whence Rutland lies at your feet. A little farther on at the left is a heap of white rock quartz where a Rutland man once mined for gold. The first turn to the left brings you in time to the half-way house, a few rods below which is one of the prettiest waterfalls in the country. A mile beyond this point is "Brewer's," where you can leave your horse and driver if you care to make the ascent on foot. You have already come seven miles, and there are three more of steep climbing before you reach the Killington House and a hearty dinner. The way lies through a dense forest, over a road that would put many a city street to shame, and well supplied with ice-cold springs along its course. As you make the ascent the air gradually becomes more rarefied, beech, birch, and hemlock give place to mountain ash, spruce, and balsam, and small game hurries out of the road as you approach. The giant trees which met over your head when you started on the three-mile climb become smaller and smaller as you near the top, until, when the house comes into view, they are little more than wind-tossed, storm-dwarfed specimens, little larger than stunted saplings. At the house are excellent accommodations during the summer, and a deep spring of water that has no superior in the world. The crest of the mountain is a fifth of a mile from the hotel, and is reached by steps built in the rocks. If you find yourself in the clouds, wait until the sun again comes forth; for as the mists lift there will appear the most magnificent mountain display that Vermont has to offer.

It is no uncommon thing for visitors to stand under a beating sun and witness a thunder-storm hundreds of feet below them. One day in August, 1894, a small cloud appeared in the west during the noon hour, and rapidly approached the base of the mountain. As it rolled on, the city of Rutland was obscured, and heavy bolts of lightning struck in the valley. On the mountain-top not a breath of air stirred. When upon the very foot of the mountain the cloud split as if by magic, and leaving a narrow slit of sunlight where the division occurred, the divided storm took separate ways. On one side was Pico and on the other was Shrewsbury. Over the tops of these mountains the storm passed, and entering the valley of the Ottauquechee left wreckage along its entire path.

If a traveller happens to be of an adventurous turn of mind and the day is yet in its knickerbockers, he may have the hardihood to reach Rutland by way of Lake Pico and the Rutland and Woodstock stage-road. In the days when the redskins inhabited the valley of the Otter and built signal fires on Killington peak and the Deer's Leap, there were two ways of reaching the mountain. One was over a trail that has since become the established road, and the other was by an ascent on the north side. The latter trail wound its way through the forest to Lake Pico, and from there to what is now Sherburne Hollow. To reach Rutland by the older of the two paths, you start from the Killington House barn and follow for a mile a well-beaten trail running in a northeasterly direction. Near a big rock the path leads off to the east in a most confusing manner, and finally becomes so indistinct that it takes the eye of a woodsman to follow it. If you possess such an eye, you will find that after following a ledge for half a mile the trail takes a northerly course, and finally brings you to the end of a wood-road, the starting-point of which is the old Plumley Mill. Should you, like many others, become confused, turn straight down the mountain-side and follow the first brook you happen to strike. This will soon join others, and either bring you out at the mill or at Lake Pico. If you come out of the woods at the mill, take the road that leads up a gentle grade, past a building on which is painted the word "Sroxu," and you will pass the lake and arrive at the stage road, after a two-mile walk. Should the brook prove to be the inlet of the lake, follow the same corduroy road to the left and you will reach the top of the mountain, after walking a mile and a half. From here to Rutland the distance is ten miles down the mountain. On such a trip it is well to carry a rifle, for should you chance to meet a black bear or Canadian lynx, the consequence to an unarmed explorer might be anything but pleasant.

A Primeval Forest Way.

(52)

DEER'S LEAP. 300 FEET ABOVE RUTLAND AND WOODSTOCK STAGE ROAD.

But should you see a bear, the safest thing to do is to take the advice of sage woodsmen and let it alone, for bear-hunting is an art the successful accomplishment of which is known only to the few.

Of the many summer resorts in the vicinity of Rutland, Lake Bomoseen is one of the most popular. Here
Lake Bomoseen. can be enjoyed pure air and spring water, and fine fishing and hunting. The lake lies in the towns of Castleton and Hubbardton, and is a pleasant drive of sixteen miles from Rutland, over a hill and valley road that has few rivals in the State. The lake is eight miles in length and in some places two miles broad, and receives its inflow from rills along its shores and springs in its bed. The lake is in the basin of Georgia or argillaceous slate, and has a quarry on one shore. There are several good hotels about the lake, and many cottages. In summer the place is the resort of city folk, but is unusually free from picnics and gatherings of that nature. In fact, Lake Bomoseen is a fashionable summer resort, and is becoming better known each season.

Clarendon and Middletown Springs. Clarendon Springs, eight miles west of Rutland, is one of the more quiet summer places, where many people spend the hot months among the Green-mountain foot-hills. The resort has no water front, but people are attracted here by the health-giving springs, from which the place takes its name. A comfortable hotel is the principal place of entertainment.

Middletown Springs, a few miles farther on, is a resort of a similar nature. The village has a slight advantage in size and hotel accommodations, it being the seat of the Montvert, one of the largest summer hostelries in the State.

West Rutland and the famous Marble Quarries. West Rutland, five miles from Rutland, is, with Proctor, the centre of the marble industry of the world. The town may be reached by carriage or by electric or steam cars, and a profitable day can be spent in and about the quarries, which are famous the world over. A visit would not be complete without making a descent into the "Sheldon" quarry. This is one of the deepest in the world, and to see the men getting out huge blocks by the aid of diamond drills one will have to leave the surface of the earth behind him and go down over two hundred feet and then follow a passage underground for some distance. The marble taken out is finished near the quarries, and each process through which the stone passes may be observed.

Nearly every one who has occasion to go to Woodstock or Stockbridge from the western side of the mountains takes stage at Rutland, and if he is bound for Woodstock he goes by way of Sherburne "Holler" and the Bridgewaters. Those
From Rutland to Woodstock. who go any other way live to regret it. The stage line to scenic-loving Vermonters is what the Alps are to the Swiss, particularly in summer, when one can scarcely afford to miss the chance of a ride in a comfortable stage over the top of the range. Sundays excepted, the stage leaves Rutland at 2.30 o'clock in the afternoon, and reaches its destination in the evening. From Rutland to Mendon the road ascends a slight incline, and from there to the summit lies through one of the wildest reaches of forest in Vermont. During the last two miles no houses will be seen, and for that matter few other signs of civilization. At the top the stage-driver will rest his horses, and will point out on the right a road leading to Lake Pico and United States Senator Proctor's shooting-box, and on the left to the Deer's Leap, a cliff rising several hundred feet above the level of the road and crowned with clumps of weather-beaten spruce trees.

The precipice is marvellously constructed by Nature, being honeycombed with dark vaults and subterranean passageways extending no man knows how far. The leap is associated with many curious traditions, and while the mountain inhabitants

BRANDON STATION.

The Deer's Leap and the Bear Caves. refuse to admit suggestions of superstition, it nevertheless remains an undisputed fact that the caverns are never visited by them. It is said that the stage road was once an Indian trail. Stories of ghosts and hobgoblins hang about the cavernous recesses, but they are seldom told by daylight. One mountaineer alleges that on a cold moon-light night, while passing the leap, the ghost of an Indian crossed his path, and making uncanny signs with his tomahawk disappeared in the direction of the caves.

Just how the cliff came by its name is a matter for conjecture, but it is said that a deer once leaped to death from the top of the precipice when chased by a party of Indians. Many a fisherman, reaching the summit at daybreak, has seen the bald eagle rest-ing in the air over rabbit runways, and then fall at a tremendous rate to the earth. The poets see in this wild manœuvre many grand things, but the mountaineers know that the eagle was simply after a breakfast.

A Bear at Close Quar-ters. In the fall of 1895 two newspaper men visited the Deer's Leap caves for the purpose of exploration. Tying their horse to a tree at the top of the mountain, the two men entered the woods and were not long in finding open-ings extending into the mountain. After rambling about for an hour or more with a dark-lantern and a camera, a passage was found entering the rock at an angle of forty-five degrees. Down this a stone was rattled and went rum-bling until the sound was lost. In the vicinity of this were many more passages, and directly at the left yawned the mouth of a large cave. Into this the two went, and after passing through many intricate passageways they ascended through a natural tunnel and found themselves well up toward the top of the cliff. From this point of vantage there could be gained a view of the road many feet below, and farther off to the east rose the line of abrupt hills at the foot of Ottauquechee river. Directly behind the explorers a cavern led straight into the mountain. One newspaper man stationed himself here while the other followed a hedgehog path to a point above the cave. Here he found a shaft, and a near-by rock when dropped into it struck with a sullen thud many feet below. No sooner had the stone reached the foot of the shaft than there was a scrambling below, and a huge bear lumbered out of the mouth of the cave within a rod of the explorer, and disappeared in the direction of the road. In less than five minutes there was a confusion of neighs and growls in the regions below, and when the newspaper men reached their team the frightened horse had succeeded in partially demolishing the carriage. A few hours later the bear was caught in a trap set by a Sherburne "Holler" man.

Lake Pico and U.S. Senator Proctor's Shooting-Box. The road leading south from the Deer's Leap to United States Senator Proctor's shooting-box lies through a forest so dense that the trees, in many instances, meet over the roadway and form, in summer, a "lovers' lane" two miles in length. The first sight of civilization is the old buildings of an abandoned logging-camp which was "struck" many years ago and moved farther back into the mountains. The lake is seen directly after leaving the old camp. It nestles in an out-of-the-way corner in the woods, two thousand two hundred feet above the sea level, and is the most remarkable natural trout-lake in the State. The club-house, a modern structure, is situated on the right of the road as you approach, and commands a fair view of the water front. The lake is as famous as it is remarkable, and, before it was "posted," was the rendezvous for the few sportsmen who knew its whereabouts. The water is nowhere more than five feet deep, but a rock may be sunk in the bed to an unknown depth. The lake is fairly alive with red and green lizards and blood-suckers, which are the only inhabitants besides the trout. No other fish can live in the water. Lake Pico finds its source in hidden openings somewhere in its filmy bottom, and in a small inlet-brook rising on the summit of Pico. The trout are as peculiar as is the formation of the lake. They average from eight to ten inches in length, and rarely exceed three-quarters of a pound in weight.

One day they will take a fly as fast as it is cast on the water, while on another thousands may be seen jumping and not one will touch the feather. They will rise aggravatingly near, take a look, and disappear from sight. One can row silently among the lily pads all day and will never so much as see a fish, yet a hundred trout may be rising within flyshot of the boat. This is extremely puzzling, unless you know the formation of the lake bed. Before the "posters" were put up, heavy baskets of fish were taken here on summer days, and twice, when the season opened in April, bushels of trout were taken through the ice.

A Land of Deer and Deer Yards. There is no place in Rutland county where game is more plentiful than in the vicinity of this lake. Deer are seen daily, and grouse and hares can be had for the shooting. The lake is on a runway from Killington to the hills west of Deer's Leap and connects two famous yards. Over this runway deer-travel may be said to be heavy.

The Plumley Mill. Beyond the posted land lies a forest broken only by the deserted Plumley Mill, which a few years ago was the scene of considerable lumbering activity. The buildings still stand and afford a good place to put up a horse for a day. From the mill to Sherburne "Holler" runs a trout brook where fish may be taken in season. The forest in the vicinity is particularly wild, and bear and lynx are often seen. One day when the old mill was in full operation a buck, angered by a terrier pup, chased a lumberman to the mill and hung about all day. On another occasion a bay lynx jumped upon a woodsman, who barely escaped with his life. In the rear of the boarding-house is an Indian orchard. In one of the trees a bear was killed one Sunday, where he was chased by the terrier pup before alluded to. F. M. Plumley, the manager of the mill, has taken fifty bears about here and on Shrewsbury mountain during the last twenty years.

Sherburne "Holler." From the top of the mountain to Sherburne "Holler" the road descends at a quick grade. At the "Holler" the driver changes horses while you eat a bountiful supper at the tavern named "Traveller's Home," with the S on the signboard painted upside down; and the trip to Bridgewater village is continued in the dusk of the evening down the Ottauquechee through a beautiful valley.

The Bridgewaters. Of all the interesting points in Bridgewater, the gold mines stand preëminent. They cannot be better described than by a writer who says:

There are a good many ways of getting to Bridgewater — "Bridgewater village" it used to be called to distinguish it from Bridgewater Corners and Bridgewater Centre and West Bridgewater and Bridgewater Hill and all the other Bridgewaters, as well as from Bridgewater in general; but the most delightful way of all is down the river from Sherburne. It is twelve miles from that village to this, and my understanding is that the world has but one finer drive of the length, and that is the one from Bridgewater to Sherburne. The up-stream journey has the advantage for the better effect of the river and mountain. Ottauquechee river is no more than a good-sized brook in Sherburne, but it never fails in beauty. You start from there Bridgewaterward down a valley straight for a long distance, at first astonishingly narrow, and the sides as steep as they well can be and support vegetation. That on one side of the stream is remarkable for its regularity and seems like a roof of living green hundreds of feet high and three miles long. Only the lower parts of the mountain-sides are cleared; the upper mountain is mostly left to forest and primeval evergreen, and birch and maples are mixed in with all sorts of younger growth in a way to give all the shades of forest green. The cleared land on the mountain-sides is used for pastures, and the cattle have such steep work that it seems as if they ought to carry spiked tails with which to brace themselves, like chimney swallows. But there is bottom land made level by time and water. The meadows spread out and make fair farms, and there the mountains shut in until there is barely room between their feet for the river and the road. In fact, the meadows run along with these breaks in such a way as to suggest an irregular string of sausages on a large scale.

It is only a little way from Bridgewater Corners, where once dwelt Josiah Josslyn, famous for his quaint philippics, to Bridgewater village, the real metropolis of the town. The village is situated at this point because of the falls of the river. The power is used by a saw-mill, grist-mill, and flannel-

LAKE DUNMORE FROM AN ELEVATION. SILVER LAKE JUST OVER THE MOUNTAIN AT THE RIGHT.

galena running across it about a foot wide and washed bright by the water. Father carried some of the galena home, borrowed a book on mineralogy, and with the help of that tried to find out what the stuff was. He finally extracted a bit of gold about as big as a pinhead. He then tried to buy the land with the brook, and after some trouble succeeded. News of the discovery went out, and many people came to look at the place and the rocks. Father sold a small undivided part, in 1854, to one Smith, of Winchester, and the two men went to mining. Both sold out in June to Payson, and work began on a larger scale. He lived in Woodstock, had a fine pair of horses to drive up here, and $4 brandy was none too good for him to drink. But he did not know much about the business and the thing stopped."

The next morning I drove to the Minore mine, the one most responsible for the excitement. I went up the road toward Sherburne, nearly three miles from Bridgewater, to Henry Tuttle's house. Mr. Tuttle has been "in" the gold excitement from the first, and yet takes a rather conservative view of things. He did not seem very enthusiastic, and I suggested that he had not caught the fever. "No," he said, " I hain't got much fever. I am too sick and feel too bad to git up much gold fever. They've had it here lots of times; fever right up."

"But there is gold here, isn't there?"

"Oh, yes; gold enough. Trouble is gittin' on't out. 'Bout like all the old banks where there was $3 in paper to $1 in silver. Put in $3 an' git $1 out."

"Isn't there gold on your farm?"

"Yes, I s'pose so; but they ain't gittin' it out."

"Doesn't anybody make anything out of these mines?"

"Oh, yes; somebody allus makes. There's so much speckerlation that somebody makes, but I've had the rumatics an' didn't sleep much las' night an' — I dunno."

"May I hitch my horse here while I walk up to the mine?"

"Sartin. Hitch right here; the hoss'll be all right. I didn't sleep much las' night and I'll go inter the house an' go to bed."

I walked across Mr. Tuttle's land and soon came to a "side hill" pasture in which I heard a peculiar hammering near a little stream that came tumbling down the hill. I went to the spot and there found two men in an irregular hole blasted out of the loose rock. One was pulverizing some rock with a sledge-hammer, while the other looked on. They were Canadians, and the pounder was evidently the boss.

"What are you doing here?" I asked.

"Gittin' out gole," answered the taciturn pounder.

"Have you really found gold here?"

"Yaas; las' wik Ah git some plee, not so verree breg though," and he went on pounding.

"You don't seem very busy here?"

"No; my man what sharp un drill, he seek. Ah guess Ah don't work verree puttee quick 'fore he come some more ; " and the pounding continued. The Canadians washed a panful of powdered rock, and at last, after several searches, the pounder indicated a shining scale the size of a pinhead.

"He's gole," he said. "He de secon' piece Ah fine." Both regarded it with much satisfaction, and they were looking at it when I left.

On the way home I saw a man in a field and stopped to talk with him.

"Mornin'."

"Do you know anything about the gold mine about here?" I asked

"Du know ? "

I repeated my question.

"Dunno nothin' about it."

"Then you haven't caught the gold fever?"

"Du know? Fever? No, I ben nockerlated."

"What?"

"I've ben nockerlated more than thirty year ago."

"How was that?"

factory, all owned by one man. There are some stores, a little church, and a small hotel, and the village is done. The old church was burned years ago and took the hotel alongside. The little tavern, on the same site, is kept by the son of the proprietor of the old inn. The old church had fallen into disuse and had somehow come to be owned by Nathan Lamb, who lived next door, with the similitude of a lamb of the four-legged kind painted white on the cast-iron gate before his door. Nathan has gone to his rest now, the cast-iron lamb has disappeared, and even the story of his offering a second-hand pulpit for sale is fast fading out.

The Famous Gold Mines of Bridgewater.

Everybody has heard of the mines. They are almost as old as those of California, and have been brought before the people times without number. It was in 1855 that the "gold fever" was first felt. Everybody was sure of getting rich off-hand, and from that day to this there has been a succession of new discoveries, new mining companies, new mining, new mills, and new failures. Every attempt, thus far, has been a failure. What successes have been made in manipulating companies in a speculative way, and "salting" mines and that sort of thing, it is impossible to say. It is said that over $1,000,000 in good money have been spent here mining. Likely enough if everything was reckoned the figure would run a good deal above that, for the business has been going on for a generation, and with many single operations of no little magnitude.

Gold Taken Out.

No one can tell how much gold has been taken out, but it might reach half the amount it cost. It has all been getting ready for things and "developing," with now and then a little metal to show. There is in the whole history no story of paying works. Still there is gold there. Good authorities say that there is gold in every town in this longitude all through the State.

The Branch.

In the summer of 1895 I paid a visit to the mines. I was told that the first man to see was Oscar F. Washburn, that lived "up the Branch," and that the mine, which once assayed from $10,000 to $70,000 a ton, was located on his farm.

"How shall I get there?"

"Well, you foller up the Branch, and jest the other side of the Branch you take the Dailey Holler road, and anybody'll tell ye where Washburn lives. 'Bout six mile."

These are the directions I got — a trifle ambiguous in spots, but clear enough when you are familiar with the local dictionary. The Branch is a stream that runs into the Otisquechee a little above "Holcook's," and is also in common speech the little village of Bridgewater Centre. So I drove up the Branch and over the Branch to the "Dailey Holler" signboard, and up the "Dailey Holler" road to Washburn's. I crossed a little bridge, turned sharply to the left, and went up a hill steeper than any prairie-bred mind could believe existed. This was geographically a little southwest of the centre of the town. Mr. Washburn was at the mill, I was told, and I followed a little path to a fence and continued through a field forty rods westward toward the mill. Directly I came in sight of an iron smokestack looking strangely out of place with its mountain surroundings, and there appeared a narrow gorge at the edge of the forest with a little tinkling stream at the bottom and the mill just on the other side. At a workhouse in the corner of the building I found Mr. Washburn and an assistant hard at work. The assistant from time to time dipped from a wooden bucket with a cast-iron spider a quantity of water with quicksilver at the bottom. This he poured into a large piece of chamois-skin held by Mr. Washburn. The water was squeezed from the skin into an iron pan and the operation was repeated.

"What are you doing?" I asked.

"Getting out gold," was the answer; and Mr. Washburn took up a wide-mouthed bottle containing an irregular lump of something resembling tinfoil crushed together.

"That's amalgam," he said, "quicksilver and gold." I then saw that there was some substance in the chamois bag, and that the squeezing operation was to separate this from the water and quicksilver. "We are just cleaning up our first batch." Mr. Washburn continued. "This is the first test with the ore." He then more fully explained the process and gave an interesting account of his mining experiences. He had lost $27,000, but was firm in the belief that he would strike metal some day. He had made a study of gold mining and was confident that there was a vein of gold running from Nova Scotia to the South.

On my way back I stopped at the "Branch," and was told by Matthew E. Kennedy how his father discovered Bridgewater gold. He said:

"No, it was not by accident. My father was always interested in minerals and in examining them. I bought the land Washburn now lives on in 1840, but did not own the lands the mines were on. My father came to visit me in August, 1841, and examined very closely some peculiar reddish rocks he found in a stone-heap on my land. He was hunting bees one day after that and followed them across the little brook, and there he saw some more of the same rock. He went home some time after, but came back and we went to take up the swarm of bees. In crossing the brook this time we saw the vein of

Caught in Shrewsbury Pond.   "NOT AN OPTICAL DELUSION."

"Took all summer. Borrered portators to git through the winter. Ain't seat of no fever."

"What do you mean by that?"

"What might your name be?"

I satisfied him, and he asked:

"Ye don't wanter buy no gold mine, do ye?"

I replied that I did not.

"Ben here long?" he queried.

"Not long enough to hear of 'nookerlation' for gold fever."

"Didn't ye never? Jullusk us not ye hain't. Best way. Some on um et didn't get nookerlated'll tell ye so. It's jes kinder a light run o' fever -- sick some. Hed to borrer portators. Kep' my farm. Ef I'd hed the reg'lar fever, I should er los' that."

"Do they get rich up there?"

"Reckon not. Now, lemme tell ye. I've ben here a tol'rable while. They've ben a diggin' gold an' trouncin' round for mor'n forty years, an' I jes' dug one summer. Rest o' the time I ben diggin' portaters. I uster hev bilbows an' pink eyes an' peachblows an' Jackson whites an' a lot ou 'm -- but they're all portaters. I ben diggin' on 'm, an' there hain't nobody ben diggin' gold thet's got ahed o' me. Take portaters an' gold an' you can give me the portaters. I've ben nookerlated an' I hain't diggin' gold. Goin' to rain. Es ole Uncle Sile Bugbee uster say, 'It's too wet to work out-doors; boys, let's go an' hoe in the gardin.'"

And so the old farmer left me.

The Trip to Woodstock. You go to Woodstock from Bridgewater and you take the stage owned and driven by "Young Bill Billin's." "There are middle-aged men," says an "east-sider," "who remember this stage-driver at work when they were children, looking exactly as he does now, for time changes his face no more than his appellation. He was 'fresh-faced Young Bill Billin's,' driving stage and saying nothing, a generation ago, and he is 'fresh-faced Young Bill Billin's,' driving stage and saying nothing, now. There was an older Bill Billin's, his father, who died a few years ago after driving stage more miles than could easily be recorded. William Billings drove stage between Woodstock and Bethel almost fifty years, and would have rounded out the half-century had not political changes put the route into other hands. 'Young Bill Billin's' lives at Woodstock and drives to Bridgewater every day of his life, carrying mail, passengers, and miscellaneous paddlodock, and doing errands. Passengers and mails excepted, he charges ten cents for carrying everything and doing anything, keeps no accounts, never makes a memorandum, and is reputed never to have forgotten anything, not even a dime."

Trout-Fishing about Rutland. Rutland is a centre for fishermen, and there is scarcely a day in summer that some man or boy does not bring in a good string. One reason for this is that Killington, Pico, and Shrewsbury are covered with ice-cold springs, the waters from which trickle down the mountain-sides into the trout-stream feeders, keeping them clear and cool in the hottest July weather. The streams from the western slopes of these mountains reach Otter creek in the vicinity of Rutland, and trout may be taken from the sources of the main streams to the base of the foot-hills. As these peaks are but a few miles from Rutland, a two hours' drive will bring one to the best brook-fishing in the county, where one may take trout from May 1 to September 1. All trout taken under six inches in length must be immediately returned to the waters in which they were caught. Fish and game wardens are notably vigilant in Vermont, and have a habit of suddenly appearing at your side while you are casting a fly, and demanding a sight of your catch. This they will surely get before they leave, and woe be unto you if by chance or intention you have retained an undersized fish.

UPPER END OF LAKE DUNMORE.

Killington, Pico, and Shrewsbury, and intermediate mountains, form the watershed of the main range in this section of Rutland county. The streams on the west side find their way to the Otter in trouting river, and those on the east side find an outlet in the Ottaquechee by means of many small brooks. Cold river, East creek, and Furnace river drain the west

The Green-Mountain Watershed. slopes. Cold river finds its source in two reaches of primeval forest. The north branch rises on Killington peak and drains the valley between that mountain and Pico. The fishing is good to " Brewer's," eight miles from Rutland. Here the stream forks into Brewer and Eddy brooks, and the trout run so small that fishing is unprofitable. The south branch rises on Shrewsbury mountain and drains the valley between the south slope of Killington, the east slope of Little Killington, and the north slope of Shrewsbury. The fishing is excellent to a point two miles above " Burditt's Mills," ten miles from Rutland. The streams meet five miles from the city and form Cold river proper. The river is fished with a bait during the month of May, and with flies from June until the season closes.

East creek proper rises in Chittenden meadows ten miles northeast of Rutland, where will be found some of the best fishing in the State. The south branch, sometimes called " Mendon river," rises in the town of Mendon, a few miles east of the city, and drains the north slope of Pico and the Mendon " basin." The two streams join in the town of Rutland, and enter the Otter below the State House of Correction.

Furnace river finds its birthplace in the North Chittenden mountains, and reaches Pittsford after a rough course through a gorge above the " Mills." The trouting is excellent for both fly and bait from the mountains to the "Mills."

Few " posters " forbid fishing on any of these streams.

The State Fish Commissioners have done much to improve fishing in Rutland county waters, by stocking the brooks with fry and fingerling trout taken from the hatchery at Roxbury.

On the last night of the session of the Vermont Legislature, in 1896, the Senate and House of Representatives **Repeal of the Deer Law.** passed the most important law affecting sportsmen's interests that has been sent to the Governor for signature since the six-inch trout bill became a law. By virtue of this statute, October, each year, will be an open month for shooting deer throughout the entire State, and as the " white flag " has not been under fire in Vermont for many years, it goes without saying that the best shooting in the East will be found here with the opening of the season in 1897. The law, as signed by the Governor, provides that only deer with antlers may be killed, and that but two may be taken by any one person in the course of a season. It prohibits the use of dogs, salt-licks, jack-lights, crusting, and traps; and allows one deer and the head, hoofs, and hide of another to be taken from the State when accompanied by the captor. The first provision is intended to protect does and young bucks.

Late in the sixties a sportsman might have hunted for a month and failed to find so much as the track of a deer, for in all parts of the State the animals had fallen prey to the traps and guns of pot hunters who paid little heed to Nature's **Why Deer are plentiful in Vermont.** laws and still less to public sentiment. About this time a party of philanthropic sportsmen residing in Rutland procured a dozen bucks and does from Dannemora, N.Y., and turned them out on the foot-hills a few miles east of Rutland. The Legislature was asked to coöperate by protecting the deer, and the request was granted, a law being enacted providing for a heavy fine for killing the animals at any time during the year. From that day until the present law was passed the statute was rigidly enforced by vigilant game wardens backed by an interested public. General sentiment was also in favor of the enforcement of the law. For several years after the deer were liberated in Rutland-county woods nothing was heard of the animals, but in time they began to multiply, and on several occasions herds were seen feeding in the mountain pastures. With ample protection the deer finally became so numerous that two years ago the inhabitants of Essex county began to complain that the animals were infesting their grain fields and ruining their crops. Eventually the farmers petitioned the Legislature for redress. Similar action was taken in Rutland county, but no relief was afforded by the General Assembly. In 1896 the farmers came together under a common flag and made good a demand for an open season.

As the animals became plentiful they seemed to realize that they were safe, and grew to be so tame that in winter they would often feed with the cattle in the barnyards. In Sherburne "Holler" there lived for several years a large buck named "Uncle Billy."

The Buck and the Deacon. The animal put in an appearance one cold December day. He established his headquarters in the sheds near the old church, and expected and usually received daily rations. When food was not placed at his disposal "Uncle Billy" would take it upon himself to make good the deficiency by stealing fodder left by horses in the stalls. For some time the old fellow was a great pet, but finally became ugly and now and then knocked down his benefactors. At length the citizens began to consider how they could rid the community of the animal and at the same time evade the law. Matters came to a crisis one Sunday morning when by a "most unholy act" the buck brought down death-dealing wrath upon his head. "Uncle Billy," who was uglier than usual that morning, caught sight of a venerable deacon on his way to church and gave chase, and the deacon entered the sanctuary in neither a dignified nor picturesque manner. This alone would have been enough, but as if to invite destruction the buck "squared off," and, landing on the church door when the parson was in the middle of his long prayer, sent the splinters flying in all directions. The next day "Uncle Billy" was found lying in the sheds with traces of Paris green in the grain box in the stall in front of him.

Deer Yards in Rutland County. There are more deer in Rutland and Essex counties than in the remaining twelve, for the reason that in these territories the forests are extensive and particularly adapted for the growth of the animal. In Essex county the enforcement of the law prohibiting the killing of deer has been comparatively lax, while the opposite is true with regard to Rutland county. It is even alleged that three members of a jury before whom an Essex-county man was brought for violation of the deer law were once entertained by a friend of the respondent and given a dinner, the principal item in the *menu* of which was Vermont venison. Though the case went against the accused, the jury failed to convict him.

The main reason why Rutland county will afford the best deer-shooting in the State in 1897 is because of the many deer-yards existing in various parts of the territory. Through the centre of the county extends the main Green-mountain range, with Killington, Pico, and Shrewsbury, three of the highest peaks, standing so closely together that there is room between their feet for small valleys only. The forests were partially cut over a few years ago, and thus the "second growth" and old timber afford feeding-ground for deer during the entire year. As there are all kinds of food to be had in a small area, the animals do not need to migrate, and thus are found in the county the year round. Killington has an altitude of 4,241 feet; Pico, 3,967 feet; Shrewsbury, 3,737 feet; Little Killington, 3,951 feet; Little Pico, 3,134 feet, and Mendon peak, 3,837 feet above the sea level. All are within an area of five miles square and within ten miles of Rutland. Thus it will be seen that of all the regions in the State where deer can be found there is none more fitted for breeding and development than this. Roads from Rutland run to all the principal points where deer will be found, and it seems probable that this city will be the centre of operations in October. Guides may be picked up either in Rutland or in the mountains, and lodging may be had at almost any farmhouse.

How to Reach the Deer "Yards." To reach the Pico deer-yards and hunting-grounds one may take the stage to Sherburne "Holler" and from there follow "the west hill" road to the old Plumley mill. By a private conveyance one can drive to the "Summit" on the stage road and turning to the right follow the Lake Pico road past the Proctor club-house to the same point. From here roads lead back into the mountains between Killington and Pico.

To get to the "yards" on the southern slope of Killington drive east over the "Notch," take the left-hand road to "Brewer's," and put up your horse. By following a mill road running east from a point a few rods north of the barn you will soon find yourself in a wild country where deer are plentiful.

Shrewsbury is somewhat less easy of access, as it lies behind Little Killington, for which it is often mistaken. To reach the mountains, drive to Noyes' mills and enter the woods from there.

A Wild Deer In a City Street. About one o'clock in the afternoon of July 16, 1895, when the streets of Rutland were full of men returning to work, a full-grown buck was seen in the lots adjacent to South Main street. All hands gave chase, and the animal was finally captured and taken to the barn of Lester Fish. Members of the Rutland Fish and Game Club were notified and orders were given for the animal's release. The deer died before the order could be carried into effect. An autopsy was performed, but no evidences of injuries were found. It is supposed that the animal had been chased by a hound, and becoming bewildered had run into the city, and had died from fright.

Many Deer In Sherburne Valley. There are probably more deer seen in Sherburne valley than in any other part of the State. A reason for this is that the valley lies between sparsely settled mountains in the very heart of the deer region. Hardly a day passes that some one does not see a deer, and the sight has of late become so common as to cause little or no remark. On Jan. 1, 1897, a deer bolted out of the woods in front of the post-office, turned down the Bridgewater road, crossed the iron bridge, turned to the left at the F. M. Plumley farm, and passing within a few feet of the house made its way into the woods on East mountain.

On another occasion a buck came into the farmyard and later leisurely trotted into the woods.

Bears and Bear-Hunting In Rutland County. Mountain forests that support and shelter deer will support and shelter bear. While the Vermont laws shield deer and invite the destruction of bear, the latter are very common in Rutland county. One cannot visit the deer-yards among the mountains east of Rutland without crossing bear-runs. The killing of bears is a regular item of sportsmen's news in these parts. Four black bears were killed in 1893 by the side of the Rutland and Woodstock stage-road, near the old Ripley mill in Mendon. For years bears have been shot or trapped for pelt and State bounty; but the Legislature of 1896 repealed the bounty law, and it is fair to assume that fewer pelts will be brought in by hunters.

A Four-Days' Bear-hunt. Bear-hunting demands great endurance and a stock of patience of almost biblical proportions. F. M. Plumley, of Sherburne, one of the most successful bear-hunters of the State, followed his first bear four days before he killed it. It was in November of the year 1872. It had been snowing, and Mr. Plumley started out with shotgun and dog for grouse or "patridges," as they are commonly called in the back districts. He started up the south slope of Shrewsbury mountain, back of his farm, and he had not gone an eighth of a mile through the forests when the dog suddenly made

LAKE DUNMORE, LOOKING WEST.   ADIRONDACKS IN THE DISTANCE.

a dash for the brush and small trees. The hunter followed, and soon came upon a beaten bear-path in the snow extending from a clump of beech trees to the top of a knoll, where the trail was lost among the low spruces. The animal had evidently been beech-nutting, and when disturbed had made for cover in a direction plainly marked by tracks.

After following the trail for a hundred rods, Mr. Plumley came upon a low ledge in a clearing, where two years before J. H. Learned had cut timber for one of the mills in the valley below the Plumley farm. Across the ledge ran a road covered with tree-tops and general *debris* well decayed after two years' exposure to sun and rain. The path ended at a point where the dog stood guard. The bear had evidently crawled under the tree-tops, and when some of these were removed the hunter discovered the mouth of a cave. Plainly enough there was but one way to gain an entrance, and this was to follow the example set by the bear and crawl in. Dropping a brace of balls into the barrel of his shotgun, Mr. Plumley got down on his hands and knees, with the muzzle of the piece pointing toward the mouth of the cave, and slowly felt his way along the damp passage. He had crawled about four rods, when a low growl in front of him, and a moment later a pair of gleaming eyes, warned him of the danger of this kind of bear-hunting. The hunter attempted to reverse his gun, but before he could do so the bear made a rush and pushed past him, jamming the man against the side of the cave in his hurried exit. At the mouth of the passage the bear was met by the dog, and although the canine did not close in upon the animal, he worried him toward the woods, and the two were twenty rods away when Mr. Plumley emerged from the cave and sent a mixed charge of shot and bullets into bruin's flank. The shot told, but failed to stop the animal, and the chase continued until sundown, when the hunter and his dog found that the bear had rounded the base of Killington, skirted Pico, and that he himself was in Mendon more than ten miles from home, as the crow flies, and more than twice that distance by road. That night the tired hunter and his dog spent in Mendon, and early the next morning Mr. Plumley, armed with a trusty rifle, set forth, this time accompanied by a man named Colburn, and the bear was chased to Cook's hill. Here Colburn, who was not up in bear-hunting, gave out, and Mr. Plumley was obliged to leave the trail long enough to return to Reuben Ranger's, in Mendon, and enlist the services of two men named Hinckley and Carey. That day the three followed the bear trail to the "Notch" four miles from Rutland, and there darkness again suspended the sport. The next day Colburn had sufficiently recovered to join in the chase, and he, together with Mr. Plumley and a man named Parker, took up the trail. The party had several shots during the day, but the distance was so great and the woods were so thick that though the balls from the Winchesters struck the animal he still kept his feet. Finally, toward nightfall bruin was brought to bay in a thick covert of spruce trees, and every man levelled his gun and pulled the trigger. Snap, snap, snap went the locks, but the balls had become loosened in the brass shells, the moisture had worked in, and the crack of the cap was the only response. Mr. Plumley now volunteered to take the bear single handed. About ten feet from the now thoroughly enraged bear was a fallen tree with just room enough under it for the animal to crawl. On this tree Mr. Plumley stationed himself, and drawing a twenty-two calibre revolver from his pocket he instructed his companions to drive the bear under the tree. Slowly the animal walked toward the spot, and when within a foot of his face Mr. Plumley levelled his revolver and, aiming at the eye, sent a ball crushing through the animal's brain.

The chase over, the party took note of their surroundings and found themselves in a wood bordering a pasture in the rear of the Plumley farm-house, and scarcely a hundred rods from the spot where the bear had been started three days before. The animal weighed three hundred pounds and measured seven feet from nose to tail.

FOREST PARK FARM
A SUMMER RESIDENCE

Proctor.

THREE miles beyond Centre Rutland and five miles beyond Rutland proper is the town of Proctor, a small but important station on the Rutland railroad. The town is the headquarters of the Vermont Marble Company and the home of United States Senator Redfield Proctor. The topography of the town resembles that of an Alpine village, and the streets are at such angles that it takes more than one visit to become familiar with the place. The village is veritably built of marble, and the stone is seen in every shape from the rough block as it is taken from the quarry to the carved specimens in the finishing rooms. In color it is a dark mottled and is exceedingly handsome. The two-thousand-horse power to run the machinery of this vast city of mills and shops is furnished by the falls of the Otter, below the residence of Senator Proctor. Above the roaring torrent hangs a suspension foot-bridge, where not only a view of the falls can be obtained, but also the valley of the stream from Proctor to Pittsford. This spot has for years been the Mecca of photographers and painters, but can hardly be considered finer than that from the railroad a quarter of a mile north of the depot. The town was originally called Sutherland Falls, after James Sutherland, an early settler.

The Head-quarters of the Marble Industry.

Pittsford.

PITTSFORD is considered by tourists to be one of the most beautifully situated towns in the State. The main village lies on a hill overlooking the valley of the Otter, and is a mile from the railroad station, which is now reached by a pleasant road of easy grade. The "Mills," an important division of the village, is a hamlet a mile southeast of its better half. The town is a good example of thrift, and is more than ordinarily progressive. Within a few years a system of water-works has been laid out which brings pure drinking-water from the famous "sand" springs and also gives ample fire-protection. It may truly be said that in this progressive age, with all its modern improvements, there is no town in Vermont which more fully retains the old New England characteristics of the early part of the century than does Pittsford. Many of the citizens are direct descendants of the Vermont pioneers, who had so much to do with weaving the history of the State, and accomplished so much for Vermont during her strife with New York. The village is becoming more and more of a summer resort, and the inhabitants, realizing the natural advantages possessed by the town, are doing all in their power to make the place attractive.

A Beautiful Village in the Valley of the Otter.

The battle-ground of Hubbardton is an easy buggy-ride from Pittsford, and as considerable attention is paid to the roads in every direction, either along this really superb valley or back on the mountains, coaching parties find the conditions for travel the very best.

The town was chartered Oct. 12, 1761, to Ephraim Doolittle and others, and was named after William Pitt, then prime minister of England. The "ford" end of the name came from the fact that at the point where the pioneers settled was a ford across Otter creek. While there is little known of the grantees, it is a matter of history that the inhabitants were a hardy set of men and took no small part in the wars of the Revolution, that of 1812, and of the Rebellion. During the days of the Revolution there were two forts in the town. There are several burying-grounds, the oldest of which is that laid out in 1785.

UPPER LLANO CATARACT SOUR LAKE ?

Eleazer Harwood was the first Congregational minister. He was not a reverend, but was chosen to preach on account of his rare judgment and personal qualities.

The ice cave of Pittsford gorge is one of the most curious sights in Vermont, and, strange as it may seem, **An Ice Cave.** one of the most unfrequented by visitors. This gorge lies between two sharp peaks situated about three miles southeast of Pittsford Mills and about half a mile from the road leading from that place to East Pittsford. The reason why the cave is rarely visited in late years is because the gorge is neither frequented by hunters nor fishermen, and is too remote and rough to entice many pleasure parties to visit it. It is said that during the warm summer months the Indians, who inhabited this region before the conquest of the white men, used to store in the ice-bound subterranean channels their fresh venison, and tales are related of pottery and arrow-heads being found there by early explorers in this region. Some who have visited the gorge have been unable to find the entrance to the vault, and have come away with the belief that the whole story is a myth, while others, who were fortunate enough to find the opening, have lacked the means or inclination to make a descent into what looked to them to be a bottomless aperture in the rocks. To learn the exact extent of this cave and to determine the falsity or truth of the various rumors connected with it, a party of three, of which one was the writer, left Rutland on Aug. 6, 1894, taking with us ropes, lanterns, and general paraphernalia for descending into the cave.

We left Rutland about four o'clock in the morning to avoid the extreme heat of the day, and taking the old **A Visit** Pittsford road turned to the right on the East Pittsford road at the school-house about six miles from Rutland. **to the Vault.** This road runs parallel to the foot-hills of the Green-mountain range, bounding the valley of the Otter on the east, and further on connects with the North Chittenden road about a mile above the Furnace flats in Pittsford on Furnace brook. At the end of this line of hills, or rather where the brook cuts through the range on its way to the creek, the peaks rise abruptly to a considerable height. Between these two sharp peaks lies the narrow gorge in which we expected to find the cave. Hitching our horse at a farmhouse, and taking our lanterns, ropes, etc., we began the ascent to the entrance to the gorge. The way lay over a rough pasture, with an incline of about four hundred feet in an eighth of a mile. By the time we gained the top the sun had risen and it was blistering hot. Finding a solitary tree, we rested beneath its shade. The view from this point was superb. Spread out at our feet lay the broad valley, with the gentle Otter gliding peacefully through on its way to Lake Champlain, and the vivid green of the meadows, punctuated by white farmhouses and clusters of red barns, with cattle grazing here and there in the pastures, made a scene of rural peace. The whole was bounded by the sombre forested mountains dwindling in the distance till they seemed to meet on either side in a narrow apex. We had no difficulty in finding the entrance to the gorge, for the opening was fully one hundred feet wide and easily discernible from our resting-place. We entered the gorge and followed it, keeping well in the centre, where the hedgehogs and rabbits had made the semblance of a path. A more wild and rocky place it would be hard to find. Throughout the entire length rocks and massive bowlders are heaped promiscuously one upon another, as though a gigantic maelstrom at some prehistoric time had suddenly subsided and left its former bed devoid of earth and water, but filled with broken remnants of a destructive age, strewn about in chaotic disorder. To this refuse cling moss and lichens, with numerous stunted trees striving for existence in the crevices between the bowlders and rocks. On either side the peaks rise abruptly, on the right to a height of one thousand seven hundred and sixty-seven feet above the sea level, and on the left to a height of one thousand three hundred feet. Climbing over the rocks and decayed trees, or crawling under the bowlders, we made

(72)

our way to the upper end of the gorge. Here on either side the cliffs rise in sheer precipices about two hundred feet high, and are backed at the further end by a semi-circular wall that slopes by a series of steps to the conjunction of the peaks beyond. It was in this rock-strewn amphitheatre that we were to look for the ice cave. Shut out from the sunlight with the exception of the noon hour, it was indeed the spot of spots to find ice in July. Looking up into the warm, deep-blue sky above, with the snow-white clouds drifting aimlessly about over the narrow gorge with its bare, cold rocks on either side, we beheld a scene worthy of a painter's brush; while below, at our feet, the gray stone, the vivid color of the grass, and the brown lichens contrasted strangely.

Soon we discovered the entrance to the cave. Hidden in a recess in the cliff, at the foot of the north precipice, it is not strange that it has been overlooked by searchers. Crawling on our hands and knees into the mouth and turning sharply to the right we found a circular hole, six feet in diameter, descending into the blackness below. From its subterranean depths **Descending the Chimney.** ascended a chill moist air that with the surroundings of the place made the flesh creep. Across the hole was thrown a log about six inches through, while from the further edge projected the top of a primitive ladder placed there by an exploring party years ago. Finding this too fragile to trust, we descended by our rope, taking a lantern with us. At the depth of thirty-five feet we came to the first landing, from which a passageway led for some distance to the east, descending at an angle of forty-five degrees. Here the air was still colder and our thermometer registered fifty degrees above zero. The rocks were, however, comparatively dry, and we failed to find water dripping from the walls as we had expected. After fastening our rope and putting on our overcoats we made our way carefully down the passageway. After proceeding about thirty feet the floor became moist and slimy, and the air gradually grew colder. Suddenly we came to an end of the channel and saw that we stood on the edge of a precipice. The roof was higher here and branched out on either side, making a passageway fifteen feet wide. Beyond this we could see nothing. Stationing one of our party here, we let ourselves down by the rope for twenty feet until we stood on the bottom, and found ourselves in the ice cave. Certainly the term "ice cave" is no misnomer, for the floor was composed of a solid bed of ice fifteen feet thick, and as hard and solid as that found in a mill-pond in February. Chunks and slabs were also strewn about, measuring between a foot and two feet in thickness. The roof sloped toward the centre from either side, until it ended in an apex fifty-five feet above our heads. The vault was seventy-six feet in length. From the main chamber branched passages leading in every direction. In most of these the aperture was too small to admit of our exploring them. Those that we did follow soon found their end in solid rock. The air in the main vault was exceedingly cold, and we found by our thermometer that the temperature at the top was forty degrees, and at the bottom near the ice thirty-one degrees above zero. Though undoubtedly the cave had been visited within ten years, we found nothing in or about the place to verify the fact. No scraps of paper or bits of rubbish were discovered, neither were there any initials scratched upon the rocks. After remaining until we were thoroughly chilled, despite our heavy clothing, we made our way with some difficulty into the outer air. A careful examination of the gorge failed to bring to light any other cave containing ice. Since this, a new ladder has been placed in the "chimney," and descent made easy and practicable. Numerous parties visited the cave in the summer of 1895, and thus far have always found ice. During the summer of 1896 a party of young ladies from New York and Boston visited the cave and ate their lunch in the main vault, cooling their lemonade with ice perhaps a century old. In explanation scientists say that the gorge is so situated that in winter it receives no sunlight, and the rocks are chilled so deep below the surface of the ground that they do not warm up with the few hours of sunshine the gorge receives in summer. It is not improbable that the whole vicinity is underlaid with ice.

A few years ago a good deal of talk was heard in Vermont concerning abandoned farms and why they did not pay. To-day many of these farms are being bought up and profitably worked. A good instance of this is found in the experience of Miss May J. Eaton, of Boston. While spending a summer in Pittsford Miss Eaton bought a small farm and a fair farm-house in the town of Chittenden, eight miles from the Pittsford station. She paid for the whole $1,000. The house was repaired at a small expense, and the farm, not including the house, was rented for $100 a year, thus bringing ten per cent. on the investment. There is a garden near the house, and plenty of fishing and hunting, and it is not improbable that a number of Boston people will in summers to come be benefited as the result of this investment.

What a Thou-sand Dollars will do in Vermont.

This is but one of the many illustrations which might be given of how a little money will go a great way in Vermont. A summer home among the Green mountains is open to any man with a small capital, for he can live here at so small an expense that it will be much cheaper than either boarding at a summer resort or remaining in the city. There are many mountain farms containing a hundred and fifty acres of wood and tillable land and a good substantial farmhouse that may be bought for $700 or $800. In Simonsville, six miles from Chester, there is a farm of one hundred acres for sale at $700. There is a good house on the farm, and it would require the outlay of $100 or more to put it in good repair. There is another farm in the same locality containing the same number of acres and a fair farmhouse and barn. This can be bought for $800. A few hundred dollars' outlay will put it in the best of condition. Simonsville is one thousand feet above the level of the sea, and besides pure air and water possesses two distinct advantages. The soil is not worn out and is superior to that found on many a valley farm. Again, owing to its altitude, the milk from cows grazing at this height above the sea level will keep much longer than that from cows on the lowlands, and it is much richer in solids.

It has been said that a man can take his family from the city to one of these farms and live cheaper and better than he can at a summer resort or at his city home. Suppose a man living in Boston with a thousand dollars at his disposal buys a Vermont mountain farm for $700 and expends $100 the first year in general repairs; he will then have $200 left with which to buy a cow, plant crops and cultivate them. At the end of the season his family of children have grown robust, he has spent practically nothing for provisions, and he has apples, potatoes, cabbages, turnips, and beets enough to supply him in his city home during the winter. For this he has paid $1,000, the interest on the money, taxes, and car-fare.

The same man taking his family to a summer resort will spend $1,000 for board, the interest on the money, and car-fare. He is minus his farm for the next year, however, and the chances are his children are not as healthy as they would have been had they spent the season on a mountain farm.

The man who buys the farm the first year returns the second year, lives for practically nothing, takes home provisions, and at the end of five years, if he has managed well, his farm will sell for $4,000. Wood properly cut in the winter from the lot on the farm will pay taxes and interest on the money invested.

On Jan. 10, 1897, a practical farmer bought a farmhouse and one hundred and eighteen acres of farm land in Mount Holly for $500. The farm is one mile from the railroad station, and includes, besides meadow and tillable land, a forest on which are nine hundred large spruce trees, eleven hundred hemlock trees, and one thousand sugar-maple trees. The farmer says that he will sell enough timber in one year to pay for the farm, that the maple trees will bring in a dollar apiece, and that at the end of three years, after living for practically nothing, he can sell the farm for $3,000.

SILVER LAKE, IN THE MOUNTAINS ABOVE LAKE DUNMORE.

In answer to a request, Dr. C. S. Caverly, President of the State Board of Health, has written for this book a short communication on the advantages of Vermont from the standpoint of a sanitarian. Dr. Caverly says:

Sanitary Advantages of Vermont described by the President of the State Board of Health.

I am asked to state some of the characteristics of that part of Vermont traversed by the Rutland railroad, from the standpoint of a sanitarian, its physical conditions, and their bearings on the health of the people. There is no doubt that the average resident of our cities, who is casting about for opportunities to spend his annual vacation, should, and usually does, scrutinize carefully the general healthfulness of the regions he proposes to visit. He wishes information about the fishing and the game, about the scenery and the hotels, and especially he wishes to know about the water, the milk-supplies, the drainage, and the general care of the sanitary conditions of the place. He will not go where he will stand a chance of getting typhoid fever or malaria, or where his child will be likely to have cholera infantum or diphtheria. In other words, in his quest for recreation and rest from the work and worries of business, he does not wish to become the victim of something worse than nervous prostration.

The region through which the Rutland railroad extends possesses a great variety of physical characteristics. From Lake Champlain on the north it passes through the rich farming-valley of the Otter, and thence climbs over the main Green-mountain range, through a sparsely settled and rugged country, abounding in natural beauties. To those seeking change, and rest, and sport, this region opens up great opportunities; to the health-seeker it is as attractive. The hardy physique and longevity proverbially characteristic of our Vermont stock, from the days of Ethan Allen and his sturdy followers, bear eloquent testimony to our invigorating air, pure water, milk, and food supplies, as well as to healthful social conditions.

Figures in proof of the healthfulness of Vermont would seem to be superfluous. Yet I venture to give such as I have at hand in regard to the general health of our people, and with regard to some individual diseases which are quite generally recognized as dependent on climatic conditions and sanitary surroundings.

The part of Vermont easily reached by this railroad includes principally Chittenden, Addison, Rutland, and Windsor counties. These four counties have an aggregate population of one hundred and thirty-four thousand seven hundred and forty-eight, of which about one-fourth live in the cities of Burlington and Rutland and their suburbs. Outside a few of the larger places the people are, of course, mostly farmers. The drainage of the west side of the Green mountains is into Lake Champlain, and on the east into the Connecticut. The sources of water-supply are numerous and abundant on the hill and mountain sides, and are utilized by most of the villages and farmhouses. The elevated portions of this territory are especially suitable during the summer for those afflicted with pulmonary complaints, being free from dust and atmospheric impurities found at lower levels and in the neighborhood of large towns. The figures here quoted are taken from the Annual Registration Reports of Vermont, and from the first "Summary of the Vital Statistics of the New England States" published in 1892 (the only one yet published).

There is probably no question that our death-rate here is lower than in any other part of New England. For ten years prior to and including 1893, it averaged 16.9 annually per thousand; that for all New England in 1892 was 19.93. Malaria is practically unknown here, except as seen in imported cases. The death-rate from cholera infantum in these four counties for ten years has been on an average 6 per 10,000 of the population per year, against 11.5 for New England in 1892; that from typhoid fever has been on an average 3.2, against 3.7 for New England; consumption 19.8, against 21.8 for New England. It is also a fact that the death-rate from this universal disease has shown a falling off during the past fifteen years of fully 33 per cent. The death-rate from diarrhœa, dysentery, and cholera morbus together in these four counties has averaged 2.5 for a decade, against 3.32 for New England in 1892.

It is unnecessary to go further into statistics. The figures only substantiate what has always been known by those familiar with our State. If the statistics of death-rates could be given for only such parts of this region as are strictly rural, and to which the transient summer resident is especially invited, the contrast would be still more striking. They include of course the whole of these four counties, with the two most thriving and populous cities of the State. To those, then, in search of health and healthful surroundings, this part of Vermont will bear investigation. It offers a first-rate chance to the business and professional man to recuperate his worn nerves, with a minimum risk to his other organs. He can feel quite sure, too, that his family will here be safe from those ailments that depend on unwholesome food, impure water and milk, and general unsanitary conditions.

C. S. Caverly, M.D.

RUTLAND, VT., April 1, 1897.

President Vermont State Board of Health.

ACROSS LAKE DUNMORE — MOUNT MOO SA LA MOO.

Brandon.

A THRIVING, busy town is Brandon, the first north of Pittsford, and withal one in which every Vermonter takes a just pride. For twenty-three years after the town was chartered, Oct. 20, 1761, the village went under the name of Neshobe, which in the Indian tongue means "double pond" or "half-way pond." There is no better-kept town in Vermont than Brandon, neither is there one in which more loyal public-spirit is manifested. The streets, lawns, and park are models of neatness, the schools are the best, and a general care is shown in all public institutions. The town, too, has its full share of business, and, though the iron foundries have gone to decay and the Howe Scale Works have long since been removed to Rutland, there is business in plenty. There are two good hotels. One is the Brandon House and the other the Douglas House. The Brandon House is the more modern of the two, and is in appointment and service one of the best in the State. The house stands on the main street facing the park, and is on the site where Jacob Simonds ran a tavern in 1786. From that day to this there has been a hotel on the original site.

A Thriving Town with Many Attractive Features.

The country around the town abounds in pleasant drives, and in summer one of the hotels, at least, is filled with city folk. Once you go to this town you get the Brandon fever, as it is called, a malady from which you never recover. Among those to become charmed with the place was H. R. C. Watson, of New York, who has built, a mile north of the village on the Salisbury road, Forest Park farm, where blooded horses and stock are kept in spacious stables. Then, too, there is the Brandon fair held on the farm, where a half-mile track has been constructed and suitable buildings put up. Every one for miles around has heard of the Brandon fair, and early each fall farmers come in and bring their families, for the fair is the event of the harvest time, and there will be no more such gayety until the winter sociable season sets in. So all go to the Brandon fair and spend two whole days looking at the mammoth pumpkins and squashes, watching the "hoss trots," and being victimized by patent-medicine venders who offer remedies for sale that are warranted to cure everything from the headache to soft corns.

Not ten minutes' walk from the centre of the village is the famous Brandon ice-well, located on the C. O. Lane farm. Ever since the well was sunk in November, 1858, ice has been taken from it at all seasons of the year. In the hottest days in July and August a bucket dropped into the well will bring up ice-cold water and fragments of ice. Many reasons have been given and many theories have been exploited as to the cause of the phenomenon, but they are so at variance with one another that to give one would be unfair to the others. At one time the Boston Natural History Society looked into the matter, but nothing came of the investigation. Nearly every tourist who goes to Brandon visits the ice-well, and all have the same story to tell regarding the finding of ice.

A Famous Ice-Well.

One of the points of historic interest is a little old house under the eaves of the Baptist church, where was born Hon. Stephen Arnold Douglas, who was made famous by his debate with Abraham Lincoln. Mr. Douglas was born April 23, 1813, and remained in Brandon until 1833, when he went West to seek fame or fortune, and so far succeeded as to be sent to the United States Senate by the State of Illinois.

Birthplace of Stephen Arnold Douglas.

After the town was organized in 1784, the inhabitants set about making laws for self-government. Many of these were exceedingly peculiar, and would to-day be as much objected to by Vermonters as is the Raines law by the people of the Empire State. One of the very first measures provided that "hoggs shall run at large provided they have a good ring in their noses."

A little later it was voted to put up stocks and a whipping-post, and they were duly set in place on the corner of what is now Park and Main streets and in front of the site now occupied by the Brandon National Bank. About this time there prevailed a great antipathy against inoculation for the prevention of smallpox, and in May, 1792, the practice was forbidden.

Incidents of Early History. In September of that year a special town-meeting was called, and after more or less debate it was voted " that all who would choose to have smallpox in Brandon by inoculation the present fall are permitted the same provided they will submit to restrictions as prescribed by the selectmen." On another occasion it was voted " that the selectmen oppose —— —— in getting a divorce." On still another occasion a town pauper was set up at public vendue to the lowest bidder for his support for one year. This was the method employed in those days to provide for town charges. Whiskey was made in large quantities, and when the bridge over Otter creek was constructed in 1792, it was voted to raise a tax " sufficient to pay Mr. James Sawyer and Elijah Avery for the rum which was expended in raising the bridge." There was a large distillery in the town run by Allen Penfield, of Pittsford, and others. The whiskey was said to be of good quality, but Penfield died of a cancer, and some people were of the opinion that this was a " punishment visited upon him for manufacturing the ardent." Perhaps the quaintest vote cast was that allowing one " Nathaniel Fish to be a district by himself to support a school peculiar to his own liking."

Eighteenth Century Humor. Humor found its way into the lives of the pioneers, and was of that dry sort so often seen in the latter part of the eighteenth century. An example is found in the reply of Deacon Joshua Field to a minister with whom he and others had become dissatisfied for assuming too much authority over his flock. One day Field and the pastor met, and the latter having heard of the dissatisfaction asked his parishioner what the cause might be. Field promptly replied, "There are many causes, but one in particular is that you lordeeue it over God's heritage." There is also a story told of Deacon Field and his wife, to the effect that when the deacon announced his intention of taking his youngest child to church for baptism his wife hid the babe in the currant bushes.

From the year 1791 comes the story of the way in which Jedidiah Winslow was disciplined for boiling sap on Sunday. From an authority of the period are taken the following memoranda :

Dea. Winslow said that he was sorry that he did it on the account of it being a grief to the minds of his brethren, but not vuing himself therein gilty of a breach of the Sabbath he insisted that he therein was himself in the way of his duty. But the Church vuing it a direct violation of the Law of god and that he might have well bin imployed in a most any other bisness — taking that with the matter of ex Ample under ConSideration — they voted not satisfied. Upon which Brother Winslow requested a CounSoll and the Church redily Complied, then proceeded and chose the West Church in Rutland for the old Church, then the Choice by vote of the Church in Jerico and the Church in Orwell and Mr. Winslow made choice of the Church of Hinesdale and the Church in Walpole.

Whether this was carried out we are not told.

Lake Dunmore. Eight miles from Brandon, at the terminus of a beautiful drive, is Lake Dunmore, one of the most romantic sheets of water in New England. The lake, with its length of five miles and width of a mile and a quarter, lies in the lap of the mountains, and is famous for its fishing and the many attractions which surround it. The spot has for years been a favorite summer resort, and has now, besides many cottages, two summer hosteries. The older of the two is the Lake Dunmore House, which will comfortably accommodate seventy-five guests. The new Mountain Springs

Hotel, one of the largest and best-appointed in the State, will house three hundred people. The lake is not only famous in itself, but the fine scenery and beautiful drives bring many people here annually. Among the places of interest are Snake mountain, Llana cascade, Mount Moo-sa-la-moo, Sunset hill, Bubbling spring, and sister resorts at Hyde manor, Silver lake, and Bread Loaf inn.

The lake took its name from Earl Dunmore, who, it is written, once looked upon the broad expanse, and conceiving the idea that his name would be a fit title for the lake to bear, prepared a christening ceremony. In the course of this he waded into the lake and standing there with the water wetting his princely legs half-way to the knees, he broke a bottle of wine, proclaiming, "Ever after, this body of water shall be called Lake Dunmore, in honor of the Earl of Dunmore." A couple of dusky savages took the bottle from the royal hand, and splitting a branch of a standing tree inserted the bottle, and the ceremony was completed.

From the mountains rising from the foot of the lake was seen, on Aug. 20, 1833, the most remarkable *mirage* ever witnessed in Vermont. Lake Champlain was observed to rise and widen out, hills appeared like islands, and Burlington, nearly fifty miles away, was seen as perfectly as though reflected in a mirror. It is supposed that the atmospheric refraction was caused by the rays of the sun passing under a long and narrow black cloud which hung in the west as the sun went down.

The Famous Cave. The most famous point in the vicinity is Green Mountain Boys' or Warner's cave, in the woods on the opposite side of the lake from the Mountain Springs Hotel. The cave, in itself, is not a large affair, but has been made so famous by that Vermont classic, Thompson's "Green Mountain Boys," that it is visited each year by thousands of persons. In his description of the cave Mr. Thompson says:

"The front of this cave consisted of a sort of natural porch, eight or ten feet in length, and of, perhaps, about half that number of feet in width, formed by a projection of the rocks above and on each side, so as to enclose the intervening space. From the centre of the area thus formed in front, an entrance, wide enough only to admit one person at a time, opened into the interior or main part of the cavern, a spacious and lofty room branching off in several dark recesses that appeared to extend far into the rocks. This cave had once been a favorite lodge with the Indians, as was evident from the flint arrow-heads, and other indications of aboriginal life, discovered in and about the place; and in late years it had been the usual resort of professional hunters, and others of the neighboring settlement, when out for more than one day on fishing and hunting excursions on the lake or its vicinity, as it afforded them comfortable quarters for the night, and such as could easily be secured from the intrusion of wild beasts, or Indians, small parties of whom, though not generally very hostile at this period, were still occasionally seen skulking among these mountains."

According to Mr. Thompson, the cave was a rendezvous for Green mountain boys during the stirring times with New York. At one time a band of these Vermont pioneers who were encamped at the cave received a warning to the effect that a New York sheriff and a *posse* were intending to surprise them that night. According to Mr. Thompson, the mountaineers laid in ambush and pitched the whole Tory party into the lake and then escaped.

Silver Lake. A short distance above Lake Dunmore lies Silver lake, with an altitude of nearly sixteen hundred feet above tide water. The lake is a beautiful sheet of pure spring-water about a mile long and half a mile wide. Of the lake and vicinity, Dr. McCosh, once president of Princeton University, said, "It is the most beautiful landscape picture in America." There is a good comfortable hotel on the lake-shore, capable of accommodating a hundred guests. Every summer this is well filled with summer people. Recently a carriage road has been built up Lookout mountain, near Brandon, and a tower seventy-five feet high will be erected on the summit, at a cost of $1,000. The view from the tower will be one of the finest in New England, it being at a point three hundred and seventy feet higher than Silver lake, eleven hundred feet higher than Lake Dunmore, and thirteen hundred feet higher than Brandon village. A large part of the Otter-creek valley, Lake Champlain and many smaller lakes, Hudson river, and the Adirondacks may be seen from the tower.

Sudbury.

EIGHT miles from Brandon, in a westerly direction, is the town of Sudbury, in the valley of the Lemon Fair. The valley is one of the richest in the State, and from one end to the other is dotted with well-kept, substantial farm-houses. The Lemon Fair is a small stream which winds its course between the low hills, and finally enters the Champlain. The name is said to be a corruption of the words "Lamentable Affair," which Ethan Allen once uttered when he crossed a bog through which the stream flows.

A Charming Spot in the Valley of the Lemon Fair. The town was chartered by Gov. Benning Wentworth, Aug. 6, 1761, and was on the old military road between Charlestown, N.H., and Crown Point. Consequently stage lines, between Canada and northern New York, and Whitehall, N.Y., and Rutland, Vt., touched here, and soon there was enough travel to warrant the erection of a tavern. The first inn was built during the latter part of the eighteenth century by one Mills, who sold out, in 1801,

Hyde Manor. to Pitt W. Hyde, for whom the town of Hyde Park, Vt., was named. Eventually the house gained a wide reputation, and in later years came into the possession of James K. Hyde, the son of the former proprietor. In 1862 the house was burned, and three years later the present commodious manor was erected. The next proprietor was the present landlord, A. W. Hyde, of Rutland, Vt., son of James K. Hyde. During recent years the manor has gained a reputation that rivals that of former days, and is considered one of the best in this section of New England. There are guests at the manor each summer, who for years have spent the warm season at this resort, and whose children have grown up under the shade of Sudbury evergreens. Besides the main building there are two cottages, a den for cards and pipes, a dancing casino, tennis courts, golf links, croquet grounds, and a livery stable. In a field in front of the house is a famous spring, reached by a broad walk half a mile in length. Over the spring is a neat house with comfortable seats. The well-kept lawn, above which tower scores of magnificent elms, maples, and birches, is dotted with shady nooks and seclusive crannies, whose rustic seats could tell many a romantic tale were they endowed with the power of speech, and which as the years have rolled by have contributed in no small way to matrimonial alliances. Such is the fact which some, at least, attest, whose parents first met at the manor. Not only do the nooks about the lawn furnish the best of spots for reading and repose, but if one has the inclination to climb a little, he will find in the rear of the house upon the hillside a number of out-of-the-way places where his book may be perused in seclusion.

Drives in any direction are sources of pleasure. Hubbardton battle-ground lies a few miles south, and Sunset lake, in the town of Benson, is about the same distance from the manor. Perhaps of all others "fourteen-mile" drive is the favorite. Leaving the manor, you go south five miles on the Bomoseen road, turn to the right three times, and return to the starting-point, after

[82]

OTTER CREEK, NEAR MIDDLEBURY, ON ITS WAY TO LAKE CHAMPLAIN.

having driven over fourteen miles of notably good road and having seen seven lakes; namely, Hortonia, Lily lake, Echo lake, Lake Bebee, Lake Bomoseen, and Long and Indian lakes.

Near the old military road on the Griffin farm is Cold spring. It is said that one day during the Revolutionary period a party of Indians passed through the town with two white prisoners, one of whom was tall and the other short. The short man, so the story goes, had received an injury to one foot, and on this one of his captors took occasion to stamp as often as practicable. When the party arrived at the spring a halt was called for rest, and the small man, becoming exasperated with the way in which he was being treated, knocked down one Indian twice his size and threw a small dog at another. For these acts of bravery he was later given his freedom.

Lake Hortonia. Lake Hortonia, a queen of sylvan waters, nestles in the bosom of the hills a mile from the manor, and is the favorite resort of the city guests during their stay. Three miles long by one broad, this sheet of water is remarkable for its depth and hidden springs that make it one of the most productive for bass-grounds in the State. Year by year the State Fish Commission has placed here thousands of black and Oswego bass, until the waters fairly teem with these gamy fish. Not only has the lake been the recipient of fish from the State, but Mr. Hyde is continually placing there adult bass.

Lake Hinkum is another sheet of water where thousands of bass are captured in a season. The lake is a forty minutes' carriage-drive from the manor, in a forest on the very top of the eastern hill, and is thought by many to be the most romantic lake of its size in the State. It is a mile long by half as broad, and is fairly black with bass. While these do not run as large as those caught in Hortonia, now and then a big one is captured. In 1896 Mr. Hyde, who owns nearly all of the shore line, erected a house here for camping parties from the manor. This house is furnished with a stove for cooking, beds, and the appliances necessary for a few days of real rusticating, and, together with a large number of boats, is for the free use of the guests of the manor.

Leicester Junction.

LEICESTER JUNCTION is a small village north of Brandon, and is the point from whence the Addison branch makes its way to Ticonderoga, N.Y. Leicester may be said to be a town without any sides, as the mountains are a considerable distance from the village, which lies in the broadening valley of the Otter. In summer it is a spot abounding in beautiful drives, and like all other Vermont villages has pure air and water. There is considerable business in the main village a short distance from the junction.

Where the Addison Branch meets the Main Line. The town was chartered in 1761, and immediately after a controversy arose as to the Salisbury and Leicester town lines. All hands took sides in the disputes and there was a general rumpus, until the matter was finally settled by the courts. The inhabitants were the same hardy settlers who built their homes in other parts of the valley, and when they finally stopped fighting and began cultivating the rich soil, good headway was made. An illustration of the hardihood of the early inhabitants is found in the first physician of the town, Dr. Elkanah Cook, a self-taught physician, possessing more than ordinary skill in bone-setting. The doctor would often travel through miles of

OVERLOOKING BRISTOL, VT. BRISTOL LAKE IN THE DISTANCE.

forest in the dead of the night to relieve some suffering patient, and as there were often no roads, he would be obliged to take a pine torch and follow a line of blazed trees.

During these days wild beasts often invaded the village, and the pioneers divided their time between tilling the soil and literally keeping the wolf from the door.

—

Whiting.

THE town of Whiting is on the Addison branch of the Rutland railroad, a few miles from Leicester Junction. The village is a small hamlet located in a broad valley, and is not far distant from the railroad station. The village consists of a street or two lined with comfortable houses; a store, two churches, a post-office, and the village is done.

The town was chartered Aug. 6, 1763, but the proprietors met for the first time at Wrentham, Mass., Oct. 6,

A Small Town in a Broad Valley. 1772. At that meeting it was voted "that half of forty-eight rights in quality and quantity be given to fifteen of the first settlers of said town" on their promise to induce thirty-three other settlers to locate there within five years. The fifteen original settlers made their "pitches." A second meeting of the proprietors was held at Pittsford, Vt., in 1783. No one was allowed to vote without showing his deed or power of attorney. They then voted that "they cheque out and make a draft of the first division lots," on the ground that the fifteen settlers had not carried out their part of the agreement, and had therefore forfeited their rights. This was a surprise to the settlers, but they arose to the occasion and submitted the following document:

> *Whereas*, a number of pretenders in the name of proprietors of Whiting have presumed to warn a proprietor's meeting in the town of Whiting to be holden at Johnathan Fassett's, Esq., in Pittsford, on the last Tuesday of this inst., May, in order to chequer out said town of Whiting for a draft of the first division lotts, contrary to the minds of the first proprietors and settlers under them and in the order of justice and equity.
>
> Now, we want to know what business a parcel of pretended land jockeys have to lay out and chequer out a town that has been settled and incorporated these seven years? By what authority or power or in whose name they presume to do this we know not. Be you who or what you will we advise you to take the counsill of the wisest of men that is to let alone contention before it is meddled with.
>
> Now in the name and behalf of the inhabitants of the town of Whiting who are legally settled and lawfully possessed of the same we strictly forbid you and publickly protest against your proceedings.
>
> AARON PERSONS
> JOHN SMITH
> JOHN WILSON
> *Selectmen.*

The matter was finally settled and the hamlet gradually grew until it reached its present proportion.

Killed in Hartford, Vt., Nov. 21, 1881, by Alexander Crowell.
Weight, 182½ lbs.; length, 7 feet.

"INTERESTING BUT NOT TROUBLESOME."

Shoreham.

THE village of Shoreham is situated about four miles from East Shoreham, where passengers leave trains on the Addison branch of the Rutland road. The town has several hamlets, including Raceville and Larrabee's Point, and with its fertile fields bordering on the Champlain is a beautiful spot in which to spend a few weeks during the hot season. There is a comfortable hotel in the town, a number of stores, several churches, and the conveniences one would expect to find in a town of one thousand three hundred and fifty inhabitants. At Raceville two woodworking industries give employment to a considerable number of men.

A Thriving Town in the Champlain Valley.

The town was chartered by Benning Wentworth, Oct. 8, 1761, and thus bears a date earlier than that of any town in Vermont west of the Green mountains and lying north of Castleton. Col. Ephraim Doolittle was the first settler, and in direct opposition to the seeming purport of his name was the hardest worker the settlement had. The town was not organized until 1786, when eighteen families made an attempt in this line feasible. In 1759 Amherst began the military road running from Charlestown, N.H., to Crown Point, N.Y., but it was some time before the work was completed. In 1789 a log school-house was built at the "Corners," and for several years the young hopefuls of the town received here thrashings and a primitive education.

The town has had several noted men and peculiar characters. Thomas Rowley, the "Green mountain poet," was born and died within the limits of Shoreham. Rowley wrote the vernacular of the times in which he lived, and made his pen a powerful instrument of warfare during the stirring days of the Revolutionary war. He was clerk of the Committee of Safety, and it is claimed that, as Ethan Allen's secretary, wrote many of the stirring paragraphs which came out over Allen's signature. In fact, Rowley more than any other man is credited with stirring the people to action during the trouble over the New Hampshire grants.

The immortal Pete Jones, found in Thompson's "Green Mountain Boys," was no other than Daniel Newton, Shoreham's most eccentric character. Thompson visited Newton several times before he wrote his book, and those who knew Pete say that Thompson's portrayal of his character was admirable. The woman Jones married fell in love in early life with a man named Tanner. Tanner went to sea, and after an absence of eleven years his betrothed, either becoming convinced of his death or believing she had waited long enough, accepted a proposal from Jones. They had been married but a year when one evening Tanner put in an appearance with all the dignity of a new-born captain, ready to take his intended to sea with him. He was obliged to become reconciled to the unexpected state of affairs, and even went so far as to forsake the ocean and live with Jones and his wife. The woman was buried between the two men in the Shoreham graveyard. Newton was as erratic as Jones. He had an idea he was going to get rich in some manner known only to himself, and on the promise to bequeath a good share of his wealth to a new academy, the institution was named after him.

A few years ago a bank in the town, located on what is known as "Pock House Point," caved in, and human skeletons were found in methodical rows. Upon investigation it was found that the spot was the burying-place for soldiers of the French war who died during an epidemic of small-pox. The town has long been a Mecca for treasure-hunters, and every summer men will be found digging holes in the ground in an unsuccessful search for buried gold. The digging must always be done at night, and an old woman must be present with her netting to keep the devil away, or a black cat must be on hand for the same purpose. Almost any summer night one can find an old woman keeping the diggers company, or a yowling cat tied to a tree near the nocturnal foragers.

Lemon Fair and the lake furnish good fishing, and it is said that the "Fair" furnishes more good pickerel than any other stream in the State.

Orwell.

NOT far from Shoreham is the town of Orwell, dropped in a rich farming district that has few if any rivals in New England, and with the village but a short distance from Lake Champlain. The main part of the hamlet is between two and three miles from the depot, where you leave the train and take a comfortable conveyance for a neat and well-appointed hotel which commands one of the finest views of the Adirondack mountains that may be had on the lake shore. In connection

A Lake-Shore Town in Addison County. with the hotel there are spacious grounds and a dancing-pavilion that see many a gay gathering in the course of the summer. The hotel is the principal place of entertainment, and many people spend the hot months here. The house is on the main street, and one coming here is soon introduced to the long line of stores which constitute the business part of the village. For a lake-shore town this has remarkably good water, the best of milk, and butter that is the pride of every farmer in the township. About the town hay-making in the broad and fertile intervales is an industry that in importance vies with the raising of fine horses, blooded cattle, and the pursuit of agriculture. Time was when Orwell was one of the greatest centres in the world for raising blooded sheep, and even now those raised here are some of the finest in the United States. For many years shipping inbred sheep to foreign countries was the principal business of many of the farmers; and to-day Australia owes her finely bred herds to Orwell and farmers living in a few other sheep-raising towns. Indeed, so highly were the sheep valued that rams have sometimes brought as much as ten thousand dollars apiece — quite a price for a little tough mutton.

If Orwell excels in natural beauty in any one particular it is in the sunsets that can be seen from any point overlooking the lake. In the words of one of the citizens, who has an eye for the picturesque, they are "worth ten dollars a foot and are cheap at that." Perhaps one of the best points of vantage to observe this evening ceremony of Dame Nature is from a prominent hill on the D. J. Vail estate, where a great sweep of the Adirondacks and lake shore gives a better effect than can be had from any other spot.

The town has had many a character since it was chartered, Aug. 8, 1763, but none were more curious than the good old clergyman who, though an ardent preacher, was addicted to the cup, and on more than one occasion partook too freely of wine. One day in particular he shocked the elders by becoming intoxicated at a celebration at Chipman's Point. Indeed, he was so badly under the weather when the party started for home that he was loaded into a wagon and a sheet was thrown over him, and he reached the town in much the same manner as a porker on his way to market. It was thought to thus shield the good man from the public eye, but the people, one and all, instantly recognized the parson by the size of his feet, which would loom up under the cotton covering.

Another character was the first white settler, John Charter, an immigrant from Scotland, who "pitched" with his family on the shore of the lake not far from Mount Independence. Charter loved solitude and hated company, and as there was not another family within many miles the old chap had things pretty much his own way until, upon the breaking out of the Revolutionary war, a body of American troops was stationed upon the mountain. The soldiers suspected, from Charter's talk and his denouncement of soldiers in general and this garrison in particular, that he was a Tory, and they annoyed the old fellow to such an extent that he finally decamped. However, he returned before Burgoyne captured Fort Ticonderoga, and when the grantees arrived he was as much of a landmark as old Independence.

The naming of the town has long remained a mystery, but it now seems probable that it was named after Lord Orwell, of England, who was interested in certain New England lands.

Mount Independence is the most historic landmark in the town. Although not over one hundred and sixty feet above the valley, the elevation commands the lake front, and during the Revolutionary war a stockade fort, together with a stone house, was built on a point nearly opposite Fort Ticonderoga. At this place a drawbridge eighty rods long was built across the water to communicate with the fortress. The place became a military station not long after Ethan Allen captured the fort, May 10, 1775, and became the headquarters for the army of the north. The old parade ground, surrounded with piles of stones, which once served as fireplaces, can be seen to-day. The elevation took its name from the fact that news of the Declaration of Independence first received in this section was announced at the garrison July 18, 1776. In April, 1776, a descent was made from the fort upon Quebec. The expedition never reached the city, being driven back by the British fleet. In July, 1777, the station fell into the hands of Burgoyne. The garrison retreated to Hubbardton and Castleton, and finally joined General Gates and assisted in the capture of Burgoyne at Stillwater.

Should you ask any one the name of the mountains you see on the opposite shore of the lake from that on which Orwell is located, they would undoubtedly tell you that they were the Adirondacks. This would be the truth, as the mountains are thus known to-day. In earlier days this name was applied only to the wilderness of mountain peaks rising within the ranges that skirt the two lakes. The ranges rising on both sides of Lake George had several names. Among them were Luzerne, Black, and Tongue. The range extending through the southern part of Schroon and about the centre of Crown Point, and ending in the cliff that overlooks Bulwagga bay, was called the Kayaderossera range. Its highest peak is Mount Pharaoh, which has an altitude of nearly four thousand feet. A third range starts at the north part of Schroon and ends at Split Rock, in the town of Essex. The highest peak is Bald mountain, in Westport. It has an altitude of about two thousand feet. A fourth range originates in Minerva, passes through Schroon and North Hudson, and ends at Willsborough bay. This was called the Boyent range. It includes Dix peak, five thousand two hundred feet high.

—

Larrabee's Point.

A Summer Resort near the Head of the Champlain.

AT Larrabee's Point there is a stopping-place for trains almost within a stone's throw of the long bridge which brings one to Ticonderoga and the New York shore of Lake Champlain. A little hamlet on the hill, within eyeshot of the railroad, is the substantial part of "Larrabee's," and a spot where many people spend the summer at one of the most delightful hotels on the lake shore. The point juts out into the lake and commands a magnificent view of a long reach of water. Fishing about here is excellent, and hunting in the woods about is good.

CHURCH OF OUR SAVIOUR, SHERBURNE.

Ticonderoga.

THERE is no place in America more interesting to the historian and lover of the antique and historic than Ticonderoga, N.Y., and its immediate vicinity. The town lies in a basin in the foot-hills of the Adirondacks at a point where Lake George ends and Lake Champlain really begins, for that part of the latter lake lying south of Ticonderoga is in truth nothing more than a creek, and was thus designated on the earlier maps. From its position it was, during the eighteenth century, the latch-string of the door of the country, and within the limits of the present town the foundation of American history was woven by men who knew not the meaning of the word fear. To-day, by reason of its position between the two great waterways, the town is the central point for tourists and others making the trip of the lakes. It is also the eastern entrance to the Schroon lake-region. Within the limits of the town the Addison branch of the Rutland railroad ends at Addison Junction, two miles from the village and within sight of the historic ruins of Fort Ticonderoga, the centre of operations during the eighteenth century. The town is reached by stage over a most beautiful road as hard as adamant and with just elevation enough to bring one within eyeshot of the lake on the west, the village on the east, and Mount Defiance in the rear and a little to the south. There are several hotels in the town, the most commodious and best appointed of which is the Burleigh, located at a commanding point on the principal thoroughfare. The hostelry is a favorite with city people both in winter and summer, and has gained a reputation of an enviable character. In summer the house is well filled with city folk who make their headquarters here and spend the days on the lakes and at the many points of interest about the town. The summer season at Ticonderoga opens in May, when the trout-fishing in Lake George begins. For several years the best trouting in this famous lake has been most prolific within three miles of the hotel, and from May until July 15. There are parties out every day. Large trout are taken daily, and it is not uncommon for fishermen to bring in fish weighing from eight to ten pounds, while now and then a sixteen-pounder is taken. Ticonderoga is a central point for these parties, because one can spend a night at the hotel, drive two miles to the lake in the morning, and returning in the evening find the accommodations of a town of four thousand inhabitants at his disposal. Parties from Boston can leave the " Hub " at eleven o'clock in the morning, arrive in Ticonderoga in time for supper, and begin fishing in the morning.

In the course of the summer many people from Massachusetts and States lying east of the lake find Ticonderoga an available point from which to reach Schroon lake. By reaching Ticonderoga by the Addison branch of the Rutland road, one can take a stage to the village, dine at the hotel, and then begin a twenty-mile drive to the lake through one of the most beautiful reaches of the Adirondack primaries, — the road lies by way of Chilson hill, up an easy grade, to the beautiful Paragon lake, once known by the name of Long pond, and from there to Pyramid lake, which stretches out in a basin formed by the mountains, — and finally to his destination, after passing Upper and Lower Paradox lakes. At all these sheets of water the best of hotel accommodations will be found, as well as excellent pickerel and bass fishing.

From Ticonderoga steamers run to all the principal points on Lake George and Lake Champlain, and in summer the town is alive with excursion, picnic, and camping parties on their way to various points of interest.

The ruins of Fort Ticonderoga, a reminiscence of the spirited days of the eighteenth century, stand on a bluff overlooking the lake, and not half a mile from the terminus of the Addison branch of the Rutland railroad.

Where the Background of American History was woven.

Fort Ticonderoga.

OLD POWDER MAGAZINE AT FORT TICONDEROGA.

EAGLE BAY, LAKE CHAMPLAIN.

BATTERY PARK, BURLINGTON.

CENTRAL PARK, BRANDON.

The old battery on the bluff is said to have been the original fort called Carillon, while back on higher ground are the walls, bastions, trenches, and barracks. Overlooking all is Mount Defiance.

Early in the eighteenth century trouble began, and did not cease until the close of the war of the Revolution. By virtue of Champlain's discovery of the lake, the French claimed the whole territory, and in 1731 built Fort Frederick, at Crown Point. The English came in, made a treaty with the Five Nations, and set up a claim on that ground. In 1755 the English sent General Johnson to drive out the obnoxious French from the Crown Point fortification, but while he was in camp on Lake George, Baron Dieskan defeated Colonel William and attacked the main army. This time he was defeated, and, sore in spirit, he retreated to Ticonderoga and built a fort, which he called Carillon. This was enlarged in 1757, and was occupied by Montcalm, who marched from here to Fort William Henry, and later returned victorious. July 8, 1758, Abercrombie, the English general, ordered an advance on the French lines about a mile back from the point, and a bloody battle ensued. Abercrombie's forces were defeated, and he at length returned to Fort William Henry. In 1759 General Amherst entrenched himself before the French lines, and the French retreated in the night to Fort Frederick, and left the fort in the possession of the English.

In 1775 Ethan Allen made his famous capture of the fort and won for himself everlasting recognition from the American people. Allen received directions from the Colony of Connecticut to capture the fort, and taking his famous Green Mountain Boys he made a forced march from Bennington, arriving on the shore opposite the fort on the evening of the ninth of May. There was trouble in procuring boats, and it was nearly morning when he, with eighty-three of the two hundred men, was landed on the west shore. Finding that day would dawn before the whole party could be gotten over, he asked all who were willing to follow him into the fort to "poise their fire-locks." Every man responded, and Allen at the head of his men entered the fort, took the garrison by surprise, and capturing a guard, ordered him to point out the quarters of Commander De La Place. In answer to his summons the commander appeared at his door with his breeches in his hand and asked by what authority Allen demanded the barracks. Allen answered him, "In the name of the Great Jehovah and the Continental Congress," and the phrase is taught in Vermont schools as is the Apostles' Creed in institutions for biblical study.

General Burgoyne laid siege to the fort in 1777, and when he placed his cannon on Mount Defiance, St. Clair, who was then commandant, abandoned it on July 4.

Salisbury.

THE town of Salisbury, four miles from Leicester Junction, is a small village in a rich farming district. Since the town was chartered, Nov. 3, 1761, it has seen many an Indian struggle and has played no small part in history during Revolutionary times. In the early days, when bear-steak and venison were a drug in the cabin larder, the inhabitants would take to fishing in Lake Dunmore and the brooks in its vicinity, and the stories told of the big catches would make the mouth of the modern angler fairly water. In the fall and spring the people of Salisbury supported themselves by trapping otters, fishers, sable, and mink. Rattlesnake-hunting was a source of some profit, as the oil was sold at a good price to the apothecary. A favorite place for this sport was Rattlesnake mountain, and in the spring, when the bark began to slip on the basswood trees, the Salisburyites would turn out *en masse* and hunt for snakes.

The Home of a Once Famous Woman.

AN EARNEST INSPECTION OF A SUMMER CAMP ON THE SHORE OF LAKE CHAMPLAIN.

From the time the town was chartered until 1796 the wrangle between the people of Salisbury and the Leicesterites took up a goodly share of valuable time, but finally, when the dispute was settled, all set about to provide for themselves more civilized conditions. A school-house was built and a teacher was engaged. All kinds of grammar were excluded as being out of place, and the rule of three was the limit in mathematical research. Many of the settlers were illiterate, and some who held important town offices could neither read nor write. In 1856 the town organized an agricultural society and held fairs. An industry in which the people took pride was their cultivation of apple orchards. The pressing of apples for cider followed, until a temperance reform ended in the destruction of many of the finest trees. Then came a reaction and a desire for more trees. They were planted, but in due time, when they bore fruit, it was found that unprincipled grafters had introduced crab-apples in place of the expensive varieties paid for.

Ann Story, of Revolutionary Fame. The most remarkable character the town ever knew was Mrs. Ann Story, the wife of Amos Story, who in 1774 came from Norwich, Conn., and "pitched" a hundred acres of land near the creek. He, with his son Solomon, built a log-house and began clearing land, when the father was killed by the falling of a tree. Upon hearing of her husband's death Mrs. Story took her family, consisting of three small boys and two girls, and started for Salisbury. Mrs. Story was a woman of large stature and muscular appearance, and possessed the strength and endurance her physique indicated. She with her children took possession of the log-house in the fall of 1775, and before many days her fame had spread far and wide. She was afraid of nothing, and immediately set about clearing the land and fortifying herself from the attacks of Indians. She could use an axe with a skill and power possessed by few of her neighbors, and in bundling and rolling logs she could surpass them all. Here amid the howl of the wolves this stout-hearted Whig woman lived and brought up her family. When the Revolutionary war broke out she built a cave underneath her house by digging a passageway from the creek to the cellar, and here spent her nights with her children. During the war the woman distinguished herself by aiding the colonists, for whom she risked her life on more than one occasion. She had many thrilling experiences, but lived to see her sons and daughters grow up and marry. Mrs. Story died April 5, 1817, at the age of seventy-five years. She was buried in Middlebury. Her cellar and house figure in Thompson's " Green Mountain Boys."

Middlebury.

A Thriving Town midway between Rutland and Burlington. MIDWAY between Rutland and Burlington is the thriving college town of Middlebury. The village is divided in the centre by Otter creek. The mountains forming a background at some little distance surround intervales of the rich farming land which caught the eye of the pioneers more than a century ago, and made the establishment of a town feasible. For a town of seventeen hundred inhabitants Middlebury has its full quota of business enterprises, and its broad streets, fine blocks, and spacious stores are the pride of all public-spirited citizens. Three hotels furnish accommodations worthy of a county-seat, and there are livery stables and the like in plenty. The town is a terminus of the stage lines to West Cornwall, Bridport, Weybridge, and Ripton, and is a point where all passenger trains on the Rutland road stop. Middlebury falls, not far below the handsome new stone bridge, furnish water-power for manufacturing concerns, and another waterfall still farther down the Otter operates the machinery of a pulp mill. If Brandon citizens are public-spirited, the people of Middlebury are treading closely on their heels. Perhaps being a college town, more than usual pride is taken in making the place attractive, but, however that may be, it is the universal verdict of those who visit the place that there is no better-kept village in the State. From its site a comprehensive view of the middle stretch of the Green-mountain range may be had. As if to provide an observation point, Nature has reared in the town a high knoll known as Chipman's hill. The elevation rises out of the valley level, with no palpable excuse, and the view from the top is unobstructed. From here the Adirondacks, the main Green-mountain and Taconic ranges may be seen. On the north is Buck mountain in Waltham, Mount Philo in Charlotte, and Camel's Hump; on the east is Potato hill in Lincoln, Bread Loaf mountain, Chittenden mountain in Chittenden, and Bull mountain in Clarendon. On the southwest may be seen the northern end of the Taconic range, which forms the Berkshire hills in Massachusetts, and in the west beyond the Champlain is Mount Defiance, back of Ticonderoga, Mount Dix, Mount Marcy, White Face, and other giants of the Adirondacks, while stretching away to the southwest Bald mountain and its companion peaks border on Lake George. Just across the valley is a sharp hill, known as Snake mountain. The hill has been a landmark since the French war, and is remarkable for a precipice on its west side commanding a view of the Champlain valley.

The town was chartered Nov. 2, 1761, but the first permanent settlements were not made until 1773, when Benjamin Smalley, John Chipman, and Gamaliel Painter, from Salisbury, Conn., built log-houses and set about clearing land. In 1766 John Chipman had cleared a few acres of land, but had built no cabin. He and fifteen adventurous spirits had come up from Salisbury, Conn., and after reaching Middlebury they branched out to "pitch" at the more favorable points. Other pioneers gradually clustered about the nucleus thus formed, and in time a community grew up. When the disastrous expedition was made by the American army into Canada in 1776, these and other border towns were open to depredations by British, Tories, and Indians, and the following year, when Burgoyne sailed up the Champlain, there was a general retreat to the fortress at Pittsford and other strongholds. It was not until 1783 that the settlers returned and, digging up what they could find of their buried treasures, began tilling the soil and repairing the damage done during their absence. In 1792 the town received a marked impetus, as the county court-house was moved here. The year following this a post-office was established, and a year later the first jail was erected.

One of the old landmarks is the Congregational church, which is a fair sample of what all such churches were at the time this was built, in 1806-9. The building was thoroughly repaired in 1851, but remains substantially as it was in the early part of the century. The Congregational society was organized in 1789, and held meetings in the court-house and other places. It was one of the first religious organizations in the county, and naturally enough it was a powerful factor in county as well as town affairs. Like every other church of the period it struggled for existence—as is shown by a vote taken in 1793 to the effect that "meetings be held in Mr. Ebenezer Summer's barn until such times as he shall fill it with hay."

Middlebury College. The importance of educational institutions impressed the people of Middlebury at an early day and considerable talk finally ended in an application for a college charter. This was granted by the Legislature when it met in Middlebury, Nov. 1, 1800, under a corporation by the name of the "President and Fellows of Middlebury College." Rev. Jeremiah Atwater, principal of the Addison-county grammar schools, was by the act constituted president. The college went into active operation under the charter, and two classes were received that fall. The first class consisted of one member named Aaron Petty. Petty was graduated with full honors two years later. From that time the college, aided by donations from the State and private individuals, grew, until to-day it has a membership of one hundred and eleven. The buildings stand on the west side of the Otter, on a hill overlooking the town and the valley. The institution is remarkable for the famous men it has turned out.

Eleven miles east of Middlebury, on a plateau sixteen hundred feet above the sea level, is Bread Loaf Inn, **Bread Loaf** one of Vermont's well-known summer resorts. The inn consists of the main hotel with cottages, a music hall and theatre, **Inn.** bowling alley, livery stables, and grounds for out-of-door sports. It has post and telegraph accommodations, and is a spot of spots to spend the summer. The property of the inn not only includes the grounds in the immediate vicinity, but many miles of trout streams and immense reaches of primeval forestry. Bread Loaf mountain is nearly four thousand feet high and is accessible from the inn. Burnt hill, three thousand three hundred feet in height, commands an extensive view of Lake Champlain, and Adirondack and Catskill mountains, and the valley of the Otter. Another point of interest is Silent cliff, which towers one thousand feet above Hancock road. Pleind lake, two thousand five hundred feet above the level of the sea, furnishes the best of boating and is a favorite place for picnickers.

Beldens and Brooksville.

BELDENS and Brooksville are two hamlets in the town of New Haven that have sprung up in the Otter-creek valley almost within the memory of man. Beldens is a small village a few miles north of Middlebury, and is the seat of an extensive marble industry made possible by the falls at this point. There is a post-office here, but no hotel, that at New Haven **Two Hamlets** answering for both places.
In the Town of Brooksville is about the size of Beldens. The soil in the valley in which these two small villages are **New Haven.** dropped is exceedingly rich and fertile, and farming and cattle-raising are the prevailing occupations.

New Haven.

THE town of New Haven is a mile and a half from New Haven Junction, a point where passengers for Bristol take the Bristol railroad, which was completed a few years ago. New Haven is a town abounding in adjacent and fertile farms, and is a picturesque spot near the foot of the Green-mountain range. A hotel furnishes good accommodations; there are a few stores, an excellent academy, a church, a livery stable and a few manufacturing interests, and the purest of water and bracing air.
The Western When the town was chartered in 1761, it included a part of what is now the city of Vergennes. In the year **Terminus of** the grant was made, John Everts, of Salisbury, Conn., was deputed to go to Portsmouth, N.H., and obtain charters for **the Bristol** two townships. He intended to locate these at what is now Rutland and Clarendon, but when he arrived he found **Railroad.** that charters covering these lands had already been granted. Everts had heard of the lower falls of Otter creek, now Vergennes, and so he obtained charters for three townships between that place and Leicester. New Haven he named after the capital of his own State. To designate the starting-point a cannon was inserted in a cleft in a rock. In later years

SHELBURNE STATION.

an iron rod was placed in the muzzle and to-day is a venerable landmark not only for New Haven and Salisbury, but for Middlebury, inasmuch as that town took its boundaries from the south line of New Haven, and Salisbury from the south line of Middlebury. Few of the original grantees ever became settlers, and little is known of the proceedings of the proprietors previous to the settlement of the town in 1769. Shortly after the settlement one Colonel Reid, who had received from the governor of New York a patent of land extending from the mouth of Otter creek to Sutherland Falls, now Proctor, drove out the settlers. This aroused the ire of Ethan Allen, and he built a fort at Vergennes and put a stop to Tory land-pilfering. From that time on the pioneers received no farther molestation from Reid. The Revolution broke out shortly after this, and the progress of the town was seriously impaired. With peace came better times, and the interrupted growth of the town was continued.

Bristol.

A BEAUTIFULLY situated Vermont town is Bristol, six and a half miles east of New Haven Junction, and at the very base of the Green-mountain range. The village is reached by the Bristol railroad, a favorite with tourists, for although the line begins at the junction and ends at Bristol, it runs through a country of great beauty.

A Busy Village in a Mountain Amphitheatre. As you alight from a Rutland railroad train, you find on the opposite side of the depot a car and locomotive that have been run down from Bristol to bring passengers, mail, and express, and for the reverse purpose of carrying more passengers, mail, and express back to Bristol. Board the comfortable car, and with little or no ado you begin your trip to the mountain's foot through a rich valley, and up a sharp ascent that grows steeper and steeper until you reach the crest of a hill. There the train shoots downward over a serpentine bed, passes the main village of New Haven, and, rounding a long curve, the little engine puffs breathlessly up another grade and makes straight for a mountain, until it seems as though you were about to pierce the very heart of it. While the train is climbing to the Bristol heights, you are for the first time introduced to the grand old mountain sentinels. On the left is North mountain, or Hog Back, as it is colloquially called, and on the south is its exact counterpart, known on the maps as South mountain, for the good reason that the Bristolites have as yet been too busy to invent a more appropriate appellation. In the gap between the two the course of New Haven river can be traced by the lower contour of the mountains, and away in the distance the forest-clad summit of a high peak lifts its head among the clouds. The elevation is known as Potato hill, and, though the mountain-top is nearly four thousand feet above the level of the sea, the name clings with such a tenacity that a new one would have small chance to live.

The village of Bristol lies at the base of Hog Back, and clings so closely to it that the great mountain overshadowing the housetops seems about to fall upon the town. The streets themselves are laid out in a methodical way, and divide off a plateau more level than one would expect to find in so rugged a country. The houses and business blocks are well built and in good repair, and a beautiful park in the centre of the village furnishes an inviting shade in the heat of summer.

Of hotels there are two, and should you find in one of them the good old lady the writer conversed with during the noon meal you will feel repaid for your visit without farther exploration. The old lady at once began a bright conversation, and in true

DRIVE THROUGH THE PINES, ON DR. WEBB'S ESTATE.

Yankee style quizzed me as to my age, business, and other minor points concerning myself. As a sort of explanatory introduction the good dame remarked that her apparent deafness was not caused, as I might be led to suppose, by affection of the ear, but rather by the unfortunate fact that her "store teeth had warped" and "rattled so when she et that she couldn't hear noways plain."

The town is well supplied with livery stables, supports schools of an enviable reputation, and furnishes its citizens and guests with water from the purest of mountain springs. There is a coffin factory in the village, where many hands are employed, but the industry tends in no way to dampen the conviviality of the people of Bristol. Should you care to visit the factory you will be courteously shown about, and if you chance to be in the proper mood you may feel inclined to leave an order to be filled *postmortem*.

Excursion points about Bristol are more varied than pen can describe, and he who goes scenery-hunting can spend a summer and then fail to go the entire rounds. There is Rattlesnake Den, Rocking Rock, Money Digger's Cave, the Devil's Cart Road, the Devil's Windpipe, the Devil's Pulpit, and the devil's almost anything that one could wish to see. Just why so many points are found with the name of his satanic majesty does not appear at once, but a person with a fertile imagination may, perhaps, obtain some tangible clue after he has passed a summer in the Bristol mountains.

Rattlesnake Den. The mysteries of Rattlesnake Den require more than one visit to fathom, and should you decide to go there prepare to spend more than one day in Bristol, for the den is on a line of other extraordinary points in this most extraordinary region. South mountain is the repository of the rocks that form the den, and while from the town they appear to be little more than a stream of pebbles they are in reality a strip of mighty bowlders extending from the base of the mountain-side half-way to the top, and are scattered over an area one hundred and fifty feet in width. The den is as barren as the desert of Sahara, and is in marked contrast with the deep green of the woods on either side and the lighter coloring of the fertile fields that stretch away in the distance. Here the robin sings no morning matin, no warbler carols his evening vespers, no ferns find foothold among the rocks, and even mosses and lichens have been banished from a territory over which hawk and eagle hold dominion, and gained in years gone by an abundant subsistence in this reptile-dedicated arena.

The Devil's Pulpit. Glance upward from the rock-strewn path along which you are picking your way and you will behold above you a vertical shaft with its base resting on the den and its apex seemingly piercing the clouds. Nearly square in form, this great bowlder, many feet in height, stands as a monument erected to Nature in honor of her great works. It is related that in the days when griffins walked the earth gigantic mastodons waded through the Champlain from the Adirondacks and, ascending to the pulpit, preached there to the inferior beings of the world. From its top the den lies at your feet, a heap of stones, and the road below, with its toy-like wagons winding here and there among the trees, is little more than a gray thread disappearing in the distance. Stop and moralize, and as the dwarf-like driver of the pigmy horses urges on his pair, the true insignificance of men ruling a vast world becomes apparent.

The Devil's Cart Road. A half-mile beyond the den and the pulpit one comes to an abrupt ravine known as the Devil's Cart Road. Here in the process of the earth's construction Nature seems to have forgotten to fill in a gap in the earth's crust some fifty yards in width and more than a hundred feet in depth. Down the slimy sides of the rocks the water trickles in summer and gives life to a luxuriant growth of evergreens along the narrow bottom.

Rocking Rock on Hog Back Mountain. Of all the remarkable geological formations in the vicinity of Bristol the most singular is Rocking Rock, on Hog Back mountain. A short climb up the side of this elevation will bring one to a convex bowlder just breaking through the surface of the ground. On the top of this are two rocks resting one upon the other and so evenly balanced on the main bowlder that the twenty and more tons may be rocked back and forth by a child. A third rock once rested on the top of the pair, but a short time ago was dislodged by woodland marauders who styled themselves sportsmen.

The Devil's Windpipe. Not far from Rocking Rock is a natural chute a hundred feet long and wide enough to admit the body of a large man. Down this rock passage one can make his way with little trouble, and have the satisfaction of knowing that he has traversed the Devil's Windpipe. It is said that the Indians firmly believed the wind songhing through the long rock-cut was nothing more nor less than the respirations of the evil one.

Ninety years ago, when Bristol was called Pocock, and bears and wolves roamed in the mountain fastnesses, there came to the village an old man, rough and uncouth in appearance, and whose native tongue none could understand. He made several purchases at the store, calling in broken English for the simple articles he needed, and offering in payment strange silver coins **A Story of Buried Treasure.** which the wary storekeeper would not accept until their value had been determined by weight. After making his purchases the old man disappeared, and at the end of a few weeks the circumstance was almost forgotten.

One day two hunters, returning from the woods, reported having found the old man digging at the base of a rough ledge on the mountain south of the town. They had questioned him as to what he was doing, and he had refused to answer. During their stay of half an hour his bead-like black eyes had never once been taken from them, nor had he moved a pace from the mouth of the small cave where he was at work. This was the story as the hunters told it, and it aroused the curiosity of the citizens of Pocock.

Follow "Little Notch" road southward from Bristol to a bridge just above the Ridley farm, turn east up a path that unwinds itself in a romantic ravine, and you will come to a wild chaotic spot, where a party of citizens from Pocock found the old man at work with a pickaxe and crowbar. The lip of the mountain overhangs the rocks and ledges scattered promiscuously about, and shuts out the light of the sun from the gloomy caverns which find their way into the heart of the mountain from coverts beneath the larger bowlders. Subterranean cataracts growl and chuckle among the recesses, and mosses and lichens cling to the damp surfaces of the rocks about. It was amid these uncanny surroundings that the gnome-like old man lived the life of a troglodyte in one of the caves and carried on untiringly his mysterious occupation. At first he refused to enter into conversation, but when the owner of the land threatened to drive him off unless he made known the object of his search, he related the story of his life. Told in broken English, the romance was not complete in all its details, but enough was learned to satisfy the visiting citizens. The man's name was De Gran, and his home was Spain. Many years ago, when he was little more than a boy, his father had brought him to America, where the two spent the summers in prospecting for gold and silver. One day, while wandering in the wilds of Vermont, they came upon a series of rough ledges on an abrupt mountain-side. Upon investigation they found a stratum of rock containing a metal which proved to be silver. The ore was very rich, and, by following natural subterranean passages far into the mountain-side, they were brought face to face with untold wealth. Taking what they could with them, the father and son went to Massachusetts and returned the next summer accompanied by a small party of Spanish miners. During the long days the little party worked ceaselessly among the rocks and caverns, and late in the fall prepared to leave. When the time came for departure the men found that of the vast wealth they had accumulated, but a comparatively small part could be carried, owing to its weight and the fact that there were few roads and no vehicles. Thus it became necessary to secrete bullion valued at over two million dollars. Near the main ledge a cave was selected and in this the treasure was placed. The entrance was walled up, made to appear as natural as possible, and then the party silently left, travelling only by night until Massachusetts was reached. It was planned to return in the spring, but during the winter a fearful epidemic caused the death of all the band but the younger De Grau. He was taken to Spain by a relative, who believed an evil spirit from the Vermont mines had presided over the untimely fate of his countrymen. Long years passed, and when white hairs of old age had replaced the raven locks of youth, De Grau first found opportunity to return to America. His memory of the place of hidden treasure was fast fading when he arrived, but his remembrance of the rock ledge and certain streams was distinct enough to make him positive that he had found the spot.

The men from Pocock believed that the old man was unsound of mind, and telling him that he might dig as long as he chose they left him. For several years he labored faithfully, occasionally coming to the village for provisions, but finally his intermittent visits ceased, and when hunters next went to the caves the old man had disappeared, leaving no clue behind him.

Time passed and the *debris* of the De Grau excavations alone told of the faith of the Spaniard. One day in the fall of 1840 a man from Bristol unearthed a curious vessel among the rocks. It would hold about a quart and was made of a substance the like of which no one had ever seen before, and the rehearsal of old stories brought about a credulity which ended in considerable excitement. In the fall of that year a party of six men from Montpelier came to Bristol and organized a stock company for the purpose of carrying on De Grau's work. Every man who put in a dollar was entitled to a hundred dollars' worth of the metal when found. Many availed themselves of the offer and operations were begun on an extensive scale. For twelve years the six men sunk shafts into the mountain-side, and though traces of gold were found not an ounce of silver was brought to light.

The treasure diggers were superstitious men and believed the treasure vault to be enchanted. Evil genii guarded the goal. A black dog with a dragon head and eyes of an octopus walked ceaselessly about the silver, and a boy with a bloody gash across his throat waved a red-hot iron staff over the hidden wealth. Now and then when an unusually heavy blast was set off the boy would be heard to sigh, and thus the faith of the party was kept up. When the treasure was reached the spirits must be exorcised or all would vanish into air. To pacify the spirits a dog must be struck on the head, and while the body was quivering in the agonies of death his blood must be burned on a flat rock where the light of the moon struck at an angle of forty-five degrees. When the fire flickered out and the embers glowed into three flashes of flame by the effects of a southwest wind, the coals must be distributed with a bare hand in a circle about the mouth of the vault.

But though a dog was always on hand he was never needed, and operations were finally suspended. To-day one finds the ledge literally honey-combed with underground passages. In the main cave is a natural chimney, beneath which a few charred sticks are scattered about. Back of the cave are the ruins of an old hut, and near by is the mouth of a shaft that descends into the earth for fifty feet and then takes a sudden turn under the mountain. Three other excavations penetrate to a far greater depth, and one has a sheer descent of one hundred feet. The spot is often visited by travellers, who know it by the name of Money Digger's Caves.

Vergennes.

THE city of Vergennes, lying just north of New Haven, is the oldest city in the Green-mountain State and the third oldest in New England. The charter antedates that of Boston, and for that matter any Massachusetts municipality, for on Oct. 28, 1788, the Legislature of Vermont saw fit to give Vergennes city privileges. The two cities older than this are New Haven and Hartford, Conn., which received their charters in 1784.

The Third Oldest City in New England. Vergennes is a beautiful city with the main part a little distance from the railroad station, from which it is reached by driving up a broad road lined with stately trees. Once in the business portion you find yourself on a thoroughfare lined with substantial houses, and at the foot of a long hill a bridge, below which are located the manufacturing interests about the falls of the Otter. You find several hotels; one, the Stevens house, being on the site of the old Painter tavern. A new hotel is the Prospect, which, from its location, commands a sweeping view of the Adirondacks and the Champlain valley, and makes a delightful spot in which to spend the summer. The city is lighted with electricity, and a new city hall of modern architecture was completed early in 1897, on the main street east of the park. Below the falls are the large buildings of the State Industrial School, where stood the United States Arsenal in the days when it was thought necessary to store ammunition in the vicinity of the lake. The buildings, which were erected in 1825, were sold to the State in 1873. From the principal business thoroughfare branch streets where stand comfortable, and in many cases elaborate, houses of ancient and modern, past and present periods of construction. The Champlain is but seven miles distant, and in the days when vessels sailed up the Otter, Vergennes was the seat of shipping interests. Of the old metropolis Hon. John D. Smith, of Vergennes, Judge of Probate for the District of Addison County, says:

Some of the attractions of Vergennes are found in its beautiful drives along the river and valley, and excursions by steamer on Lake Champlain, with its shores dotted with cottages and camps, and its waters abounding in good fish. Again, the romances of its history are interesting events to follow. Among these are the first attempt to build a saw-mill, which, when completed, was by force taken possession of by Colonel Reid, under a New York grant, which ignored the rights of the New Hampshire settlers; the rally of the settlers on the lake-shore to expel Colonel Reid's men and reinstate the original owners; a second foray of Colonel Reid regaining possession, and later the sudden appearance of Ethan Allen and the Green Mountain Boys, embellished in Thompson's "Green Mountain Boys;" a fort built by Ethan Allen and his party; the departure of the settlers when Burgoyne came up the lake; the return of the settlers in 1783-'84; and later the freak of Ethan Allen in making a city about the falls, thinking it the most promising place in Vermont for a large metropolis; and in 1807 and '8 the building of furnaces by the Monkton Iron Company, which later cast balls for McDonough's fleet.

The late President Dwight, of Yale University, visited Vergennes in 1798, and said of its scenery: " From the cupola of this building [the old court-house once used for a State house] a very notable prospect was presented to us. Eastward we beheld the Green mountains, stretching little less than one hundred miles from north to south. Westward three ranges rising in parallel ridges beyond Lake Champlain, the second higher than the first, and the third towering above the second, extended in the same direction through a distance equally great. The loftiness of these elevations; the wild variety of their summits, here arched, now waving, now obtusely, now acutely conical, and now disclaiming all approach to any regular figure; the gloomy extent of the forests which overspread their bosoms; the valley between them extending over a breadth of thirty, forty, and fifty miles, and the magnificent lake at their bottom, constituted a scene of grandeur and sublimity rarely paralleled on this side of the Atlantic."

Until recently little has been known of the history of older Vergennes. Even Mrs. Hemenway failed to gather substantial data, and for the few facts which find their way into this brief sketch the writer is almost wholly indebted to Judge Smith, who is probably the only person living who can give a reliable history of the doings of Vergennes citizens of the eighteenth century.

During the French war, from 1755 to 1760, soldiers and scouting parties discovered a rich hunting and farming territory in the vicinity of what is now Vergennes, and, as the land was cheap, many of an adventurous spirit settled here. Sixty towns were chartered in 1761. Among them were Panton, New Haven, and Ferrisburgh, the three from which Vergennes was made. In May, 1785, Ethan Allen was in New York city, and in conversation with Hector St. John De Crevecœur, the French consul, cited the advantages of present location of Vergennes, and was positive that a site containing the combination of a tremendous waterfall and a navigable river entering the Champlain, together with rich fields, could not fail to become in time the greatest city in Vermont. The consul was of a like opinion, and in this connection suggested that Vermont show her gratitude to the French patriots of the Revolutionary war by naming some of the new towns after noted Frenchmen. Subsequently the new city was named after Count De Vergennes, French minister for foreign affairs. The village grew steadily even before it was chartered, and at the time the necessary document was issued there were several saw-mills, a grist-mill, and a small forge in operation. More than this, the town had several gambrel-roofed frame houses, pot-ash establishments, blacksmith shops, and an indispensable brewery. For a time it seemed that the expectations of Ethan Allen would materialize, and in 1790 with a boom came a general expectancy that Vergennes was destined to become a great inland metropolis. Lawyers, business men, and men of letters flocked to the city and built houses, farmers settled on the outskirts, and men of enterprise utilized the falls of the Otter. Among the distinguished men who made their homes here were Enoch Woodbridge, for many years Chief Justice of the Supreme Court of Vermont ; Samuel Hitchcock, appointed by President John Adams to be Judge of the District and Circuit Courts of the United States for Vermont ; Roswell Hopkins, for fourteen years Secretary of the State of Vermont ; Amos Marsh, several times Speaker of the Vermont Legislature ; David Edmonds, whom Senator Prentis declared to be " the most eloquent man I ever heard speak," and many others.

About this time the first church was organized, but there was little regular preaching until 1792, when Daniel Clark Saunders, A.M., served as preacher for several months. Says Judge Smith :

The learned doctor's idea of rapid settlement would hardly satisfy a modern man in the present age, and possibly the doctor's successors might not like the way preaching was paid for in his day, if we may judge from the following vote passed in town meeting March 28, 1792 : " Voted to raise the sum of thirty pounds on the list of the year 1792, one-fifth part in cash, the remainder in cattle or grain at the market price, to be expended in hiring preaching the ensuing summer."

Though the city was incorporated in 1788, the charter required that it should elect no city officers until 1794. Among the first officers was Roswell Hopkins, a man of great attainments. In the county clerk's office is a book, on the fly-leaf of which was written by him the following :

" My friends, some deference is due   " I, of Vergennes, am alderman ;
To every man, both me and you ;   Yes, more, a common councilman.
But this respect in due proportion   In the office of the county clerk I am put,
Pay to every man as is his station.   And clerk of the county clerk to boot.

SHELBURNE FARMS YACHT ANCHORAGE, LAKE CHAMPLAIN.

In April, 1797, a stock company was formed for the purpose of erecting a court-house. The building was completed in time for the meeting of the Legislature, Oct. 11, 1798, and stood near the present town-house. During the session a delegation of Indian chiefs from Canada came to ask the State for compensation for their lands, which they claimed extended from the Canadian line to Ticonderoga. Nothing came of the request, but the Legislature gave the redskins a hundred dollars as a token of friendship. Mathew Lyon was one of the remarkable men of the day. Of him Judge Smith says :

He was a very able and prominent Irish politician of Fairhaven, who came to this country a poor boy at thirteen years of age, and was bound out in Connecticut to pay the cost of his passage. He was once arrested for trial under the alien and sedition law, and by the United States Circuit Court, sitting in Rutland in October, 1798, was sentenced to four months' imprisonment and to pay a fine of one thousand dollars, with costs. He had been elected to Congress in 1796, and at the next election in September, 1798, there was no choice ; but in December following Lyon was elected while in jail. At the conclusion of his trial in October he expected to be confined in the Rutland jail, but the United States Marshal was a bitter political opponent of Lyon's, and it is said lived in Vergennes. He took Lyon to Vergennes jail, where he treated him with great rigor. Lyon's friends from Fairhaven sent him a stove for use in the jail. Lyon's term of imprisonment ended Feb. 9, 1799, and it was expected that he would be rearrested ; but having been elected to Congress, he, as soon as the door opened, proclaimed himself on his way to Congress, and thus made it unlawful to arrest him. There was, however, intense excitement throughout the district as the time for his liberation approached. He was a man to have warm and devoted friends and bitter enemies, and the natural instincts of Vermonters for free speech and a free press had been outraged, and they seemed anxious to enter their protest against political persecution.

This contribution to the Rutland " Herald " is reprinted in " Governor and Council," Vol. IV. :

At the time of his [Lyon's] imprisonment in Vergennes under the odious sedition law, passed by Congress during the Federal administration of John Adams, when he had stayed out in prison the term of his commitment of four months, and nothing remained but the payment of the thousand dollars' fine to entitle him to his liberty, it was found that the marshal of the State, whose sympathies and preferences were strongly with the Federal party and against Lyon, would stickle about receiving the fine in any other than money that was of legal tender, and in that case it might be difficult to procure the specie. Most of the gold then in circulation was of foreign coin which passed at an uncertain value according to its weight, which often varied by different weighers, and was therefore not a legal tender. It was known that Mr. Lyon while in prison had issued frequent publications, therein discussing and sometimes censuring the measures of the Federal administration, and that if any protest could be made for continuing his imprisonment and thereby prevent his taking his seat in Congress, to which he had been reflected while in prison, the marshal would not hesitate to resort to it. It was further ascertained that if the fine was paid the marshal intended to rearrest him for subsequent publications. Therefore to secure his liberty so that he could take his seat in Congress, which had already convened, Mr. Apollos Austin, a resident citizen of Orwell and a man of wealth, at his own expense and trouble procured the thousand dollars in silver coin, and on the day that Mr. Lyon's imprisonment expired, Mr. Austin, with the entire body of Republicans in Orwell, nearly every man went to Vergennes, where a like spirit brought together some thousands of Republicans from other parts of the district and State, in order, probably, to overcome the authorities from rearresting. Mr. Austin was not, however, permitted to pay the money he had brought. All claimed the privilege of bearing a part, and one dollar each was the maximum they would allow any one individual to pay. One gentleman from North Carolina, a staunch Republican, was so zealously anxious for the release of Mr. Lyon from prison, that he might take his seat in Congress, at that time nearly equally divided by the two great political parties, came all the way on horseback from North Carolina with the thousand dollars in gold to pay the fine, supposing that in Vermont, then new and comparatively poor, the resources of the people were not sufficiently ample to meet the exigency. Having paid the fine, the friends of Mr. Lyon immediately took him into a sleigh, followed and proceeded by a concourse of teams, loaded with political friends of Lyon, which reached from Vergennes, as they traversed Otter creek upon the ice, nearly to Middlebury, from which place a large number continued to bear him company to the State line at Hampton, N.Y., where they took leave of him and wished him God-speed on to Congress.

Lyon was a red-headed, freckled little Irishman, with a temper to match. He held a lieutenant's commission in 1776, and was once court-martialled and made to ride a wooden sword about camp, thereby gaining the derisive title of the "Knight of the Wooden Sword." While in Congress in 1798 he had a personal affray with Rodger Griswold, of Connecticut. During a debate Griswold twitted Lyon with the "wooden sword" story, and Lyon spit in his face. A fight was prevented by friends of the men, but both narrowly missed expulsion.

In 1813 the fleet of vessels later commanded by Lieut. Thomas McDonough was fitted out in Vergennes, and spent the following summer on the lake, with well-known results. It is said that McDonough's flag-ship, the "Saratoga," was built in forty days. McDonough hurried the building of the ship, saying that he wanted it only for one or two engagements, and he did not care if the best of timber was not put into her.

One of the men of the day was Gen. Samuel Strong, who, in consideration of his services at Plattsburgh, in 1814, was presented by the State of New York with a sword of exquisite workmanship. The large house built by General Strong stands to-day on one of Vergennes' principal streets, where the hundredth anniversary of the building was celebrated in October, 1896, by Hon. John O. Smith, a direct descendant. The building is the oldest unaltered house in the city.

The Ferrisburghs.

FERRISBURGH and North Ferrisburgh are villages at which trains on the Rutland road stop, and in the course of the summer leave and take on many people who are drawn here by the beautiful valley of the Champlain in which the villages lie. North-bound passengers leave the Otter at Vergennes and immediately the road slopes to the lake-shore, and as you pass the Ferrisburghs and enter the fertile reaches of country beyond you get your first glimpse of the lake. In Ferrisburgh there **Two Hamlets** are two churches, stores, and a few manufacturers, and in North Ferrisburgh there is a good hotel, in addition to two **in the Valley** churches and other evidences of a village.

of the Cham- Ferrisburgh was chartered June 25, 1762, but it appears from all accounts that there was no town organiza-**plain.** tion until 1785 or 1786. At this time there was a road as far north as Pittsford, but from there to Vergennes there was nothing but marked trees to guide whosoever should be bound for Ferrisburgh and the lake region. But later when a road was constructed, pioneers began to settle in the vicinity, and it was not long before the settlement became of considerable size. With the advance of civilization a church was built, and the pioneers were, perhaps, more punctual in attending the services held there than are their descendants to-day. One good man, who had no sled, fitted runners to a trundle bed and took his wife and children to church in it every Sunday while the snow was on the ground. The contrivance suited a double purpose, for when a mountain squall descended upon the church-going party a quilt would be drawn over the load, and thus they would keep snugly out of reach of snow and wind until the church door was reached.

The records of the doings of Ferrisburghites were burned. An account of the "calamity" reads as follows:

A COPY OF THE ACCOUNT OF TIMOTHY ROGERS, HAVING HIS RITINGS BOUNT.

Know all men by these presens that yesterday which was the sekont day of the 10 month I timothy Rogers of ferrisburgh was a moving from Hotin bay in ferrisburgh to letill orlor erik Joris and as I went by wartor I did not git up the Bay till about mid nite and my wife and five childorn and one woman peggy smith by name and one child was all in an open bote and it was a dark rany time we landid about a quartor of a mild from the hous som of the hands went up and got fir when they got down agane the fire was so rad out we cindild some fir by the side of a tree To his barks that the famaly mite se a lkill to walk up to the house for my wife was sik I led hir by the hand this morning Being the 3 day of the 10 m 1785 about son rise one of my men came and told me the tree by which the fir was kindled was bornt down and bornt up a large chist of droys that was pauki as full as it cold be off cloths and Ritings of grate importans I spose I had about forty donds for about Six Thousand acors of land som on Record and som not notes and bonds for about two thousand dolars and all the proprietors Records som other gods was bornt with all the cloths only what we had on these woughk names who air here sind ar setain witaesis to the same for they helpi me move and seen the fire of the same this 3d of the 10 m 1785 likewise they san the heaps of Riting in their proper shaps bornt to ashes

TIMOTHY ROGERS

SILAS BINGHAM
AMOS CASTLIN
ZIMMY HILL
STEPHEN RYCE JUN

At the foot of the page is written, "go to tother leaf forud page 21."
On the page referred to, the following is recorded, viz.:

Rutland county s wallingford Janary ye 28th A.D. 1786 personly aperd Timothy Rogers and gave his Afformation to the truth of the within writting depsition to before me

ABARHAM JACKSON just of pens

alorson county Ferrisburgh september the 24 day 1791 this sastafys that timothy Rogers being cold apon by the request of the select men of ferrisburgh to giv acoupt of the proprietors Records and said timothy perd with the foregoing to show that said Records was destroyed in October 1785

AIHL TOMSON asistant judg

the abov being don as apora was thought best for me to Record the same therefore was Recorded in proprietors Book page 21 thu 50 of the 9 m 1791
By me Timothy Rogers proprietors Clark.

Charlotte.

THE town of Charlotte on the shore of the Champlain is a village abounding in the picturesque and the historic, and is withal a beautiful spot wherein to spend a summer. The town was chartered June 24, 1762, but it was some years after this that a permanent settlement was perfected. In those days it was more difficult for a family to move from Massachusetts to Vermont than it is now to go from New York to San Francisco, and the development of the town was necessarily slow.

CITY OF BURLINGTON IN THE DISTANCE.

A Historic Town on the Shore of Lake Champlain. The larger number of the earlier inhabitants made their way to Vermont by way of Lake Champlain, while still others made the trip on horseback, following blazed trees during the last part of their way. During the early days of the town bear, deer, panthers, and other wild animals were common, too plentiful in fact for the comfort and safety of the inhabitants. Beavers were also numerous, and on several intervales can still be seen traces of dams built by these intelligent rodents.

Before the jail was built the town, in common with others, had its whipping-post and stocks. On one occasion a stranger came to the village and stole a cow from Capt. James Hill. He was duly tried for the theft, and being convicted, was sentenced to receive nine lashes and to pay the costs of the court. The corporal part of the punishment was administered by Constable Clark, and when the matter of costs was brought up all the officers of the court except Judge Daniel W. Griswold remitted their fees. The prisoner had no money, and in order to make things square the judge obliged the culprit to cut wood for him.

With regard to the temperance of the village a writer says:

Intemperance was a terrible scourge to the town, as was to be expected for the reason that the town was cursed with three distilleries and blessed with as extensive and fruitful orchards as any portion of the State. It also contained about a dozen taverns — all floodgates of rum and ruin. The lives of numbers of prominent citizens were marred and their deaths enveloped in a gloom by this destructive vice. But when the temperance reform commenced influential men in the town rallied to its support and carried it forward to triumphant success.

Early in the history of Charlotte the fossil of a prehistoric monster was exhumed and placed in the State House at Montpelier. The following "Observation to a Whail" was written by Miss Julia Pepper, of Montpelier, who in those days was considered something of a "poess":

Dug up in Sharlot, Vt., and now on exorbishon at the Stait Hous.

Big Reptile! Did you expect
To rub out your foot tracks by
The Trall of your Ab Domen,
So that Hager couldn't find you?
Ef so, you're sold — Great Blubber!
He knew your hand rtin, soon's
He see it! Better not jump'd
Outer the ark, quite
So much in a hurry.
Pr'aps you's ridin on an Ice Burg
And stopt to warm to Brandon
By a Lignite fire,

Or may be
You considered Lake Shamplane
Was the Pacific Oshun! Great
Setashus Mammalila Aint
You took in? Mounted on
Paddles how'd you expect to travil
I sh'd like to now, on the Clay
Called Plistersoon? Goss yuu
Felt some like a flsh out or water
Throw'd up by Joner on to
Dry Land. Ichthyosorrus,
Farwel.

Shelburne.

THE town of Shelburne, eight miles from Burlington, is in reality a thriving suburb of the Queen City, with the village on the east of the prettiest station on the Rutland railroad, and the estate of Dr. W. Seward Webb on the west. The hamlet is not unlike other Vermont villages of a corresponding size, and furnishes the accommodations found in such a place. Shelburne is marked by two distinct features that have made it famous. One is its scenery and the other is the Webb estate, one of the most notable country seats in the land.

The Home of Dr. W. Seward Webb. The estate has been named Shelburne farms, and is the legal residence of Dr. Webb. The name is happily applied, as the estate is composed of several large farms separated into divisions, each one of which is a farm by itself; yet the component parts, taken together, comprise a unit complete in every detail, and similar to the model country estates found in England and Scotland. The original purchase made in 1888 consisted of about one thousand four hundred acres, but since then enough has been added to bring the total up to the three-thousand mark. Sundays excepted, the farms are open to visitors, and are worth a trip from San Francisco to see. If one intends to make a tour of the grounds and take in everything there is to see, he had best make his plans to remain more than one day; for besides covering thirty miles of road, mostly macadamized, one will inspect buildings in which more than a day can be spent with profit.

Shelburne Farms.

About a quarter of a mile west of the depot a picket fence on either side of the broad road marks the beginning of the farms, and from there to the offices and working barns a drive of a mile and three-quarters will bring one in touch with a glimpse of Lake Champlain and fields punctuated with copse and woodland left as nature designed them. The offices and working barns, naturally the first on the course of inspection, form a hollow square on a hillside, and are surmounted with a tower and clock. The barns might be termed the middle-division buildings, for they are a mile and a half from the mansion and greenhouses on one hand, and over half a mile from the dairy and stock barns on the other. About this square, built in semi-mediæval fashion, are the offices, blacksmith-shop, store-house, tool-house, carpenter-shop, varnish-room, fire-department, mule-stables, and cottages for the employees. In the office, where the business of the estate is transacted under a perfected system, is the telephone exchange connecting the various buildings, as well as Burlington and other cities. In the fire-station is a hose-cart, by the side of which are horses trained to take their places under spring harnesses at the tap of a gong connected with a telephone alarm-system. All about the barns many men are ceaselessly at work during the day, and a visit to this part of the estate will give one something of an idea of the extent to which work is carried on in this beautiful city, isolated on the most beautiful spot on the eastern shore of the Champlain.

A little to the south of these barns is a road leading to the dairy and the stock barn, the largest building of its kind to be found anywhere. In the interior of the barn is a "ring" for the exercising of hackneys, which are famous throughout America. About the sides of this arena are stables capable of accommodating over one hundred horses.

A short distance from this point are the cow stables and the model dairy that form an interesting and instructive feature of the farm. From the barns where the cows are kept it is but a stone's throw to the dairy itself, and if one is anxious to see the inside workings of one of the best butter manufactories in America he has but to step in here. The churning is done by steam, and the cream is separated from the milk by a "separator" operated by the same power. In connection with the dairy is a neat cottage where the superintendent lives.

To visitors the mansion is of course the most general point of interest. It is located on a promontory jutting out into the lake, and one could search for many years and fail to find a more suitable spot to erect a residence covering fifteen thousand square feet and containing over one hundred and fifty rooms. From the lake-side the water stretches to the foot of the Adirondacks beyond the New York shore five miles away, while in an opposite direction the more sombre Green-mountain range recedes in the distance. Valcour Island, the waters west of which were made memorable by Benedict Arnold's battle with the British, lies a little to the north, and still farther away the spires of Plattsburgh can be seen on any clear day. In the vicinity of the house are coach stables, an electric-light station, and a power-house where water for an immense system is pumped from the lake to a retaining pond many feet above the lake level. Beyond all are the great greenhouses, and gardens, and cottages of the men who are employed about this section of the farm.

The estate has a shore line six and a half miles in extent, and forms the lake-side boundary for sheep pastures, reaches of woodland, and rich intervales. Over one hundred and twenty thousand trees have been set out since the first purchase was made, and these are already becoming of considerable size.

Connected with the farm is a large aviary where English pheasants have been propagated for several years. These pheasants are liberated as soon as they are able to care for themselves, and while some remain on the farm others migrate and are now found from the Canadian line to Bennington county. The Legislature has been asked to protect the birds until the year 1900, and such a law has been enacted.

Burlington.

O N the sunset slope of a terraced hill that finds its foot in the waters of Lake Champlain lies the city of Burlington, the Naples of New England and the queen of Vermont cities. A city of homes, of charities, and of institutions of learning, this metropolis of the Green mountains has never ceased to grow and flourish since the musical language of the Iroquois gave place to the harsher notes of the white man's tongue.

The " Queen City" of Vermont. Long before the days of Samuel de Champlain the Algonquins realized the advantageous location of what is now the site of the city of Burlington, and made the spot their home. Still later the Iroquois drove out the Algonquins, and they, too, finding the place a good one, built a village there. But before Champlain made his voyage of discovery the tribe moved farther up the lake that bears his name, and when the famous discoverer arrived there was little to tell of former inhabitants save pottery and arrowheads strewn about the shore. One hundred and twenty-two years later the French began settling at the southern end of the lake, and in 1734 three *seigniories* were granted, extending from Shelburne to Appletree bay. The French were at length driven out by the English, and on June 7, 1763, the charter of Burlington was granted by Benning Wentworth, Governor of New Hampshire. The settlement grew, and on Feb. 21, 1865, the town became a city. Now on the site where the Algonquins and Iroquois built their wigwams stand buildings of architectural beauty; commodious hotels have taken the place of the old-time taverns; electric roads follow the lines of the streets, and a city of eighteen thousand inhabitants has replaced the Indian village and French seigniories.

The Burlington of to-day takes pride in her fine residences, in her broad streets, her parks and her public institutions, and

A "LAZY DAY" ON LAKE CHAMPLAIN.

in the city itself which individual pride and public spirit have done so much to build up. Of parks there are three, aggregating an area of twenty acres. City Hall, Battery, and College parks are all that can be desired by a recreation-loving people who are notably fond of out-of-door enjoyments. The city's public buildings are many, and are built in a smart style which the date of construction would not in all cases seem to warrant. Among the more notable buildings are City Hall, the Fletcher Free Library, the United States Custom House and Post-office, the County Court House, and the University of Vermont buildings, including the Billings Library.

Burlington may justly take pride in her residences, for there is scarcely a street in the town which does not display some choice bit of architecture. This is particularly true of Main, South Willard, Pearl, Prospect, Williams, and South Williams streets, which are as broad and well-paved thoroughfares as are found in a much larger city. It was of Burlington that Edward Everett Hale once said:

> I remember the moment when I arrived there, when the magnificent range of Green mountains, white with snow as they had been through the day, were tinged with the crimson of the setting sun: and as I turned west to look upon the clouds of sunset, the sun himself was sinking behind the broken range of the Adirondack mountains. Between was the white ice of the frozen lake, and so far as Nature had anything to offer to the eye I had certainly never seen in forty years of travel any position chosen for a city more likely to impress the traveller as remarkable, and to linger always in his memory.

Burlington is a city of charities as well as a city of homes, and is known far and wide for its eleemosynary institutions. Preëminent among them stands the Mary Fletcher Hospital, founded in 1876 by Miss Mary M. Fletcher, at a cost of over $200,000. The buildings are an ornament to the city, and the institution is a godsend to those in need of medical aid. In 1885, on the death of Miss Fletcher, the hospital came into possession of the larger part of her estate, and has now free beds and $340,000 as a maintenance fund. The buildings are located on the crest of a hill not far from the University of Vermont, the site of sites for such an institution.

Another charity is the Home for Destitute Children, founded in 1865 by the efforts of Miss Lucia T. Wheeler. Since that time the buildings on Shelburne street have been enlarged, and to-day many are the little wayfarers who are given here their first start in life.

The Howard Relief Society, chartered in 1884, has made begging in Burlington entirely unnecessary, and has taken under its protecting wing many a needy person. In 1888 the society built the Louisa Howard Mission House, on the corner of Pearl and Clark streets, and in 1891 a large hall for an industrial school was constructed.

In 1886 a House for Aged Women was chartered by the Legislature, and four years later a permanent home was founded on St. Paul street.

A Home for Friendless Women was chartered in 1890, and in 1891 a building was erected on Shelburne street overlooking the lake.

The Burlington Cancer Relief Association, the Adams Mission House, and St. Joseph's Providence Orphan Asylum are other benevolent enterprises supported by the public-spirited citizens of the Queen City.

In the way of recreation the city is well supplied. There is fishing in the lake, sports in the field, and hunting in the woods. Burlington is particularly well situated for boating. The Lake Champlain Yacht Club, one of the largest organizations of its kind

RUTLAND ROUTE GREEN MOUNTAIN FLYER SOLID VESTIBULE TRAIN.

in America, has a membership of over two hundred, and a handsome building on the lake-shore, where on more than one occasion social Burlington has helped make life gay in this metropolis.

Burlington's Educational Interests. The city's educational interests echo the sentiments of the pilgrim forefathers, who in matter of relative importance placed schools next to the house of worship. As a college town Burlington takes a just pride in the University of Vermont. The college was chartered Nov. 3, 1791, a year after Vermont was admitted to the Union. The buildings are situated on College Hill overlooking the lake and the city, and the site lacks none of that inspiration which is so much built upon in selecting a location for a college. The buildings include the main structure, the Museum and Park Gallery of Art, the Billings Library, one of the most elegant structures of its kind in America, and the gift of Frederick Billings, of Woodstock, and the Science and Converse Buildings recently erected. Besides these there are the faculty residences, and last, but not least, the dining-hall. In the rear of all is the campus, where the students indulge in games in the spring, and which in the fall is converted into a "gridiron," where the same students maul one another, and struggle for the pig-skin and glory.

Bishop Hopkins Hall for young women is another institution of learning, and the Vermont Episcopal Institute for boys and young men is one more added to the list. The institute is situated on Rock point, two miles north of the city, on the shores of the lake, and is an ideal place.

Carriage-Drives and Boat-Rides. From its situation it naturally follows that Burlington is favorably located for both delightful drives and boat-rides. For a drive which will be a source of never-ending pleasure, one may visit Red rocks, Rock point, Queen City park, Appletree bay, the Winooski-river valley, the Twin bridges, Essex junction, Malletts bay, Cedar beach, Shelburne, Mount Mansfield, or Camel's hump, or many another place of interest not set forth here.

Camel's Hump and Mt. Mansfield. Camel's hump, twenty miles southeast of Burlington, may be reached by a pleasant carriage-drive to the last habitation. From there to the top the distance is four and a half miles up the sides of a rugged mountain, and if one does not care to spend a night in the woods he had best procure a guide. When the summit is reached, four thousand and eighty-three feet above the level of the sea, a magnificent view is gained of the Champlain, the valley, and the mountains beyond.

Mount Mansfield, over four thousand feet above tide water, is one of the most famous mountains in New England. To reach the peak by carriage you drive through Essex junction, Essex centre, Jericho corners, and Jericho village, and finally come to the half-way house, where you leave your conveyance and make the remaining mile and a half on foot if you desire a taste of mountain climbing. In 1892 a landslide occurred on the mountain-side, and now to reach the top you go from the half-way house by a wood road to the path of the slide, and continue in its course to the summit, half-way between the "nose" and the "chin." The view from the peak is all that one can desire, and is said to be superior to that from Mount Washington.

Cedar Beach. In the town of Charlotte, fourteen miles from Burlington, is Cedar beach, one of the prettiest spots on the lake-shore. The beach may be reached by the old stage-road running through Charlotte, which brings one within eyeshot of Shelburne farms. Go from Burlington four miles on the Shelburne road, turn to the right and follow a good road, and you will soon find yourself at this delightful place. There are several other ways of reaching this beach.

A LAKE CHAMPLAIN STEAMER ROUNDING THE BREAKWATER AT BURLINGTON.

Island Towns on Lake Champlain. If you care to visit the picturesque islands you can do no better than drive to Grand isle or South or North Hero. The two islands were originally called La Grand isle, but later forsook their French name in honor of Ethan and Ira Allen, two Vermont heroes. The island towns may be reached by way of Winooski and Sunderland Hollow. At the Iodine Springs House you find an apology for a signboard, and turning to the left across Lamoille river you pass over Sandbar bridge, and once on the island direct your course to South Hero, and here amid the most picturesque surroundings you can dine before continuing farther or returning to Burlington.

Malletts Bay. A drive of five miles from the Queen City will bring you to Malletts bay, which is reached either by the village of Winooski, or North avenue and the Heineberg bridge. The bay is a charming spot, and is but two miles from Thompson's point, one of the prettiest reaches of shore along the lake.

High Bridge. Still another point of interest is High bridge, an old-fashioned structure which has not yet fallen prey to the lovers of modern architecture. To reach the bridge, leave Burlington through Chase and Grove streets, take the Patchen road and then a woodway on the left, and return by way of Winooski after you have seen the bridge and covered several miles over a good road running through a beautiful country.

Other Points of Interest. If you are in Burlington for a few hours only, and desire a short drive, you can go to Appletree point, Rock point, or Queen City park. The latter, on the lake-shore two miles south of the city, is a noted summer campground. During the summer the spot is alive with campers who spend the warm season in comfortable cottages dotting the lake-shore. The camp is particularly well situated as regards boating, in which a lively interest is taken. Ever since the camp was established, the various meetings which have been held here have attracted people from all over the East, particularly when, as is often the case, noted speakers are heard. Just around the point are Red rocks, where one of the finest views of the lake and Shelburne bay may be had.

—

Lake Champlain.

AT the base of the Adirondacks and Green mountains lies Lake Champlain, which with Lake George is the most beautiful of all waterways of the East. With a navigable length of one hundred and twenty miles and a breadth varying from forty rods to fifteen miles, with its fifty and more islands dotting a surface surrounded by densely wooded shores, this great inland body of water is fast becoming the greatest summer abode on the American continent. Connected as it is with the Hudson river by the Champlain canal, and the St. Lawrence by the Richelieu river, the lake has become the parent body of a great ship-highway between New York harbor on the south and the Gulf of St. Lawrence on the north. Passenger steamers pass to and fro, stop at the docks along the way, and drop and take on passengers bent on business and on pleasure.

From a scenic point of view there is but one body of water in the world that rivals Lake Champlain. Lake George, on the south, too well known to be described here, is the pearl of all inland waters that America has to offer to her scenery-loving people. The lake is within easy reach of any point on the Champlain, and if the tourist cares to take the grandest trip that Nature has laid out for her children, he has but to board a steamer at Burlington and continue through Lake George.

For the grandeur of its scenery Lake Champlain places its main reliance upon the Adirondack mountains, which, if geologists tell us aright, are the oldest lands on earth. Before the highest peaks in the Himalayas or the Andes broke the surface of the waste of waters of prehistoric times, we are told that *Tahawas*, now called Mount Marcy, appeared above the deep. The completion of the valley occurred later in the Silurian period, when the Green mountains rose above the waters. Years passed, and with them the archean and quaternary periods, and still later the ice age. Then, when Nature had completed her great handiwork and unfolded a valley of wealth and beauty, the human eye rested upon it, and seeing that it was good the Indian came and made his home here. Who he was or from whence he came we do not know; what battles were fought and won we can only guess; but from the days antedating history there come to us relics of the tribes who lived upon the lake-shore. Then came the days of which we have a knowledge, and we find about the wooded shores the wigwams of the powerful Iroquois, whose tools were made of stone, whose heart was carved from flint, and who in cunning could have tutored a Macchiavelli. More than this, we find in this red warrior, whose name inspired terror from the Canadas to the Hudson, a people so far advanced in civilization as to form a tribal union. With the realization of the value of the white man's motto, "United we stand, divided we fall," they put into execution that soundest of principles, and by blood relationship founded the "Five Nations," and held the valley until the superior intelligence of the white man wrested it from them. The five tribes making the five component parts of the "Five Nations" consisted of the *Mohawks*, *Oneidas*, *Onondagas*, *Cayugas*, and *Senecas*, who by their wonderful method of self-government built up what was the most powerful Indian organization of which we have knowledge in the northern regions of America. The Iroquois were a nation in which ferocity, ambition, and pride were given equal birthrights. These three characteristics, developed for no man knows how long, built up a nation, not only of warriors who knew no fear, but statesmen, whose eloquence was heard in the council-house in the valley of the Onondaga. It was here in this Indian House of Commons that the ambassadors of the "Five Nations" were received and given audience, and where, according to tradition, Hi-a-wa-tha founded the union. The legends of the tribe tell us that after completing his work this great statesman made his final speech, and, rising in the air in a snow-white canoe, was seen no more.

" Thus departed Hi-a-wa-tha,   Of the North-West Wind, Kee-way-din,
Hi-a-wa-tha the beloved,   To the islands of the blessed,
In the glory of the sunset,   To the kingdom of Po-ne-mah,
In the purple mists of evening;   To the land of the Hereafter."
To the regions of the Home Wind,

The first record we have of Lake Champlain was on July 4, 1609, when Samuel de Champlain with two companions and a party of Huron and Algonquin warriors from Quebec entered the waters of the lake then known as *Caniaudere-guaraute*. This in the Indian tongue meant The-Lake-that-is-the-Gate-of-the-Country. The expedition passed Long island, Isle La Motte, Grand isle, and Cumberland head, and went to the southern part, where was fired "that shot which changed the history of America." But the scene has changed now. The same mountains rise to meet the sky, the same rivers continue their ceaseless course toward the lake, and the same islands rest upon its bosom. But the Indian village with its wigwams and dusky warriors has disappeared, the canoe of bark no longer glides noiselessly upon the surface of the water, and the war-cry of the Iroquois has been hushed forever. In place of all this the traveller who to-day visits Lake Champlain finds stately mansions where the tepees once stood, boats of steam mark the wake of the birch-bark canoe, and the whistle of the locomotive proclaims that civilization has replaced riot and bloodshed.

The redskin has gone, but he has left behind him relics that tell of his existence. Indications of Indian settlements are found at Malletts bay and at South Hero near Sandbar. Flint chips and earthenware are picked up here and at many other points along the shore. On the western side of the lake stone weapons, pottery implements, and ornaments are found, and even ovens and fireplaces are discerned here and there. The largest village was probably located where Plattsburgh now stands.

The whites did not permanently settle upon the lake-shore until 1730, when the French located there. From that time until their evacuation in 1760 there was little attempt at colonizing. The principal civilizing influences brought to bear during this period and for some years previous to 1730 were accomplished by the Dutch traders at Fort Orange, now Albany, N.Y. These men by their honesty gained the confidence of the Iroquois and exercised a considerable control over them. To the influence of these Dutch traders is in no small degree due the present occupancy of the lake region by the English-speaking race. The English followed the Dutch in acquiring rights, and by the treaty of Utrecht, in 1713, the French finally recognized the "Five Nations," subject to the dominion of Great Britain. The French knew the advantages to be derived from establishing posts on the lake-shore, and a colony was located at Chimney Point on the Vermont side, and a fort was built at Crown Point. In 1755 the English began an attempt to expel the French, and finally succeeded in 1759. Better days came with the retreat of the banner of Carillon, and English colonization was made comparatively easy. The pioneers began to settle in the fertile valley, particularly on the Vermont side, where the first villages found birth at the mouths of Lamoille and Onion (Winooski) rivers and Otter creek. Willsborough and Skenesboro, the latter now Whitehall, N.Y., were also settled about this time. Claim conflicts between New York and New Hampshire ensued. In 1777 Burgoyne entered the valley, and the land was again the scene of rapine and death. The difficulties were not fully settled until Vermont was admitted to the Union, March 4, 1791.

Steam navigation on the lake began in 1807, when Fulton's "Clermont" was floated. She was the fifth steamer that the world had seen, and with her came a new era in Champlain navigation. The "Vermont" was launched two years later and began regular trips between Whitehall, Burlington, and St. Johns. Other boats were built, and in 1823 the Champlain canal opened communication with New York. Three years later the Champlain Transportation Company was organized. Says a recent writer:

This was the golden period of passenger traffic on Lake Champlain. In 1849 the Rutland and Burlington and Central Vermont railroads were opened, and the Ogdensburg the following year. The railroads gradually encroached on the business of the boats, but the two night and two day boats, the "United States," "Francis Saltus," "Burlington," and "Whitehall," were kept intact till 1852. In the latter year the trip was shortened by making the northern terminus House's Point, connecting with the railroads there. Three steamboats, "Canada," "America," and "United States," performed the service up to 1874. The trip was then further shortened by starting from Ticonderoga on the south, the "Vermont" and "Adirondack" doing service. This arrangement ended on the opening of the Delaware and Hudson railroad on the west side of the lake in 1875, while the night line was discontinued, and the "Vermont" did the service of the entire line, which was again shortened to end at Plattsburgh on the north. The "Adirondack" was dismantled. The ferry trip, which has been kept up constantly, was performed by the "A. Williams" from 1872 to 1888, when a new steel boat, the "Chateaugay," took her place. The Champlain Transportation Company's fleet now consists of the "Vermont," "Chateaugay," "A. Williams," and "Mariquita." The "Vermont," a large and elegant steamer, makes the daily round trip between Plattsburgh and Ticonderoga, calling at all ports. The "Chateaugay" is used on the "ferry," the shorter and more frequent trips across the lake, to the islands, and south to Westport. The "A. Williams" is used for a spare boat and for excursions, and the "Mariquita" for service about the company's docks, and for chartering to private parties.

ROCK POINT, LAKE CHAMPLAIN, NEAR BURLINGTON.

Some of Champlain's Greater Islands. The largest islands in the lake are at the northern end. The three possessing the largest territories are North Hero, South Hero, and Isle La Motte. The latter took its name from the Frenchman De La Mothe. The three largest islands along the New York shore are Crab island, near Plattsburgh, Valcour island, and Schuyler island, near Port Kent. Crab island was the headquarters of the American fleet before the naval battles. Schuyler island was occupied by the French while they were on their way to Crown Point before Abercrombie's attack in 1767. Near the west shore of Valcour island occurred the naval battle in 1776, between Benedict Arnold and the British. A century later it was used as an experiment station for socialism.

Chimney Point. A spot of historical interest and natural beauty is Chimney Point on the Vermont side of the lower end of the lake, almost opposite Port Henry. The most prominent points of interest here are the ruins of the old French fort, and what is left of Benedict Arnold's flagship "Congress," which was sunk in what is now Arnold's bay. Directly across the lake on the New York shore are the walls of Fort Frederick.

Chimney Point was settled by the French, who had built the village now ruined by the fortunes of war, evacuated and left homes destroyed by flame, until only a chimney now and then remained to tell the tale. Thus the point received its name, and when Amherst arrived with his English army there was little to indicate the French thrift that had once flourished here.

The point is formed by two streams, North and South creeks, which find their way to the lake through the Vermont foot-hills, leaving the narrow neck of land to slope gently into the water. The lake really terminates in Bullwagga bay, and the old maps call the stretch from Crown Point to Whitehall Wood's creek. The lake at Chimney Point is not over a quarter of a mile wide, and with its natural surroundings is a most beautiful spot, and is visited by many persons in the course of the summer. The point is the property of Judge M. F. Barnes and J. W. Wright. The house in which Judge Barnes lives was partly constructed from material taken from the adjacent fort, and is one of the old landmarks.

History says that when General Burgoyne arrived at the point from Fort Frederick and found the fortifications abandoned he divided his army for his attack upon Ticonderoga, and landed here his German forces under Riedesel, Breyman, Spicht, and Baum, and then moved up to Five Mile Point. The objective point was Albany, as it was thought that if Burgoyne could meet General St. Leger from the west and General Howe from the south, the colonists would be divided by a veritable trocha. The battle of Bennington, however, made the execution of the manœuvre an utter impossibility.

General Gates established a continental navy-yard at Chimney Point in 1776, when the Americans and British were fighting for the possession of the lake. This fleet, when completed, was placed in command of Benedict Arnold, and after a few days' drill in the stretch of water between the point and Bullwagga bay, he sailed north to meet the British. In the meantime Captain Pringle, of the British navy, had gotten as far south as Valcour island. Arnold retreated in the night, and when he was nearing Chimney Point and found that he would be overtaken, he covered his squadron with his flagship, and later, in order to prevent her from being taken by the British, she was run ashore a few miles north of the point and blown up.

The Adirondacks and How to Reach them. The line of the Rutland railroad, together with the Champlain Transportation Company's fleet of passenger steamers, provides a most delightful way of reaching the heart of the Adirondacks. The southern gateway is reached with facility by way of the Addison branch and a carriage-drive from Ticonderoga, N.Y.; the eastern, by way of steamer from Burlington to Port Kent, and thence by rail and carriage; and the northern, by way of steamer to Plattsburgh, and the Chateaugay or Delaware and Hudson Canal Company's railroads from that point. The steamers provided by the Champlain Transportation Company are models of lake craft, and are provided with accommodation calculated to meet every want. The morning boat from Port Henry arrives in Burlington in time to take passengers from the Rutland Railroad Company's north-bound afternoon mail train and drop them at Port Kent, Bluff Point, or Plattsburgh, as they may elect. Hotel Champlain, at Bluff Point, is the most elaborate summer hostelry on the lake-shore, and is too well known to need either description or commendation. From the heights overlooking the broad expanse of water, dotted with its islands large and small, the spot is one of the most delightful at which to spend a hot night. The boats are, however, provided with spacious state-rooms, and are at the disposal of those who choose to spend a night at anchor.

One bound for the lake region or the mountains may take an early evening train at Plattsburgh, and by the time the owls have begun their nocturnal love-making he will find himself at Loon lake, Saranac or Lake Placid, or at any intermediate point at which he may desire to limber his fly-rod. Short drives into the deeper woods will bring one to the haunts of the whip-poor-will and the white-throated sparrow, that sweetest of all night songsters. A morning train performs a similar service, should one wish to spend the night at Hotel Champlain or aboard the boat.

An afternoon steamer from Plattsburgh touches Burlington and will leave one at Essex, West Port, Port Henry, or Ticonderoga, from whence the lake region can be reached by rail and carriage. From West Port a good road running due west touches Elizabethtown, Keene post-office, and North Elba before reaching Lake Placid and adjacent waters. En route, the road skirts the feet of Cobble hill, Knoblock, Tripod, and Baxter mountains, and follows the lake line between Pitch Off and Long Pond mountains, and finally arrives at Round pond before crossing the west branch of Ausable river near the town of Elba. The road west from Port Henry touches North Hudson and winds through intricate passes to the Ausable lakes. The route from Ticonderoga runs west to Paradox lake, and turning to the south makes Schroon lake its terminus.

—

Conclusion.

THE writer has spoken at length of some of the points of interest along the line of the Rutland railroad, and before closing this souvenir edition would bring to notice in a brief way other points of interest one would naturally come in contact with in taking the direct route from Boston or New York to Montreal, or vice versa.

Points of Interest along the Line of Connecting Road. North-bound passengers over the Rutland road will, after leaving Burlington, find themselves skirting Lake Champlain and reaches of lowland dotted with farmhouses and meadows, and punctuated now and then with a bit of forest. Across the lake to the west the Adirondack sentinels guard a broad expanse of water, while to the east, peaks of the Green-mountain range rise in bold relief against the sky. From Burlington to Highgate the proximity of the lake makes possible a land of summer homes distant from the cares of civilization, yet within easy reach of the principal cities of the East, through the medium of the railroad. Lake-fishing is more than ordinarily good in this vicinity, and as a ground for duck, grouse, and woodcock hunting the place is justly famous.

North of Burlington the first stop of importance is that made at Essex Junction, through which the main line of the Central Vermont passes on its way from St. Johns to New London. Essex may be said to be dropped on an isolated prairie, so flat is the land about the banks of the Winooski river, which winds through the town and on to the lake with many a subtle bend and charming spot marking its course. And by the way, when one speaks of Essex he can but be reminded of the poet Phelps, whose description of the place, though not particularly flattering, has nevertheless become a Franklin-county classic.

North of Essex the village of Milton at the falls of the Lamoille river has become well known to the tourist. While there is nothing to mark the hamlet in itself, the great falls, not far from the railroad, have given the town an enviable individuality that can be best accounted for by a visit. For a distance of not more than fifty rods the river is precipitated more than one hundred and fifty feet, forming a water-power of great capacity. Nine miles west of Milton station one will find Camp Watson, on the shore of Lake Champlain, where it was established and for many years maintained by the late Hiram Atkins, of Montpelier.

At Georgia the line of the railroad lies along an elevation from which a remarkably fine view of the lake may be had, and then descends to St. Albans, where the headquarters of the Central Vermont are located. Lately incorporated as a city, this little metropolis possesses advantages one would scarce expect to find in a place of its size, and offers many an inducement to summer tourists. The city has an altitude of four hundred feet above the lake, and is a place of no small consequence. The city and surrounding country abound in drives made doubly attractive by the lake on one hand and the foot-hills on the other.

North from St. Albans fast trains will carry you to Highgate Springs and across the Canadian border, through St. Johns in the province of Quebec, to the city of Montreal on the historic St. Lawrence; and you will find yourself in a country where the queen of England holds sway, and where English names give place to those of a French savor.

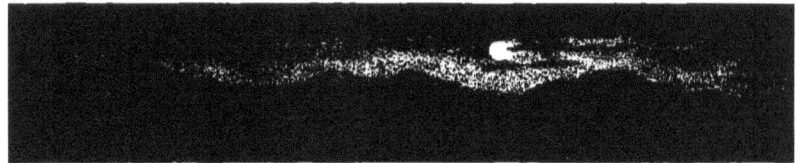

Synopsis of Vermont Fish and Game Laws.

Game - When not to be killed.

	PENALTIES.		PENALTIES.
*Deer — November 1 to October 1	$100 00 each.	birds and setting of snares at any time prohibited	$10 00 each.
Rabbits, between May 1 and September 1	5 00 "	Insectivorous and song birds, not to be killed at any time	5 00 "
Woodcock, quail, wild duck, wild goose, and plover, between January 1 and September 1,	10 00 "	Shipping game unaccompanied by owners prohibited	25 00 "
Ruffed grouse (partridge), between January 1 and September 15	10 00 "		
Sharp-tailed grouse, pinnated grouse, capercailzie, black game, ptarmigan, or pheasant, not before January 1, 1900	25 00 "		
Trapping, snaring, and netting above-mentioned			

* During the month of October, the open deer season, only bucks with horns can be taken. One deer and the head, hoofs, and hide of another can be taken from the State when accompanied by the captor. One person can take two deer in each season and no more. Hounding, crusting, salt-licks, jack-lights, and trapping are prohibited.

Fish — When not to be taken.

	PENALTIES.		PENALTIES.
Black bass — between January 1 and June 15	$5 00 each.	Taking black bass, muskallonge, pike, pickerel, or wall-eyed pike (pike perch), except by angling or on the ice, and then with not more than fifteen tended lines	$5 00 each.
When taken less than ten inches in length must be immediately returned to the waters from which taken; not more than	10 00 "		
Wall-eyed pike or pike perch, white perch, or muskallonge, between April 15 and June 15, except in Lake Champlain, where these fish may be taken with hook and line throughout the year	5 00 "	Fishing through the ice in waters inhabited by trout or land-locked salmon	10 00 "
		The use of set-lines, fishing-otters, or trawls, and all kinds of nets, punished by forfeiture and fine of	100 00
Trout, land-locked salmon, salmon trout, or 'longe, between September 1 and May 1; not more than	10 00 "	The use of set-lines not exceeding seventy-five feet in length and seines is legal in Lake Champlain when written authority is obtained from the fish and game commissioners.	
Trout, land-locked salmon and salmon trout, or 'longe, when taken less than six inches in length must be immediately returned, with least possible injury, to waters from which taken; not more than	10 00 "	The use of gunpowder or other explosives for killing fish punishable by fine of $100, to which may be added imprisonment for ninety days.	
Taking trout, land-locked salmon, salmon trout, or 'longe, except by angling	5 00 "	Exception — pickerel may be shot, with a gun held to the shoulder, from March 15 to May 1, except in Lakes Bomoseen and St. Catherine, or Lemon Fair and Syms' ponds, or tributaries to these waters.	

Possession of the above-mentioned fish and game during their respective close seasons punishable by fine.

[127]

Green Mountain and Lake Champlain.

Resorts, Hotels, Boarding Houses, and Private Residences, Entertaining Summer Visitors.

Distance from Station.	No. of Guests.	Name of Place, Railroad Station.	Rate per Week.
		Ausable Chasm, N.Y.	
40 rods.		Lake View House.	$2.50 per day. For rate per week apply to W. H. Tracy, Mgr.
		Baldwin, N.Y.	
		Grand Ave. Hotel.	$2.00 per day. For rate per week apply to J. T. Jones, Mgr.
		Milburne Hall.	$1.00 to $3.00 per day. For rate per week apply to C. H. O. Craigie.
		Bellows Falls, Vt.	
50 rods.	40	Commercial House.	$8.00.
12 miles (P.O., Grafton).	45	Grafton Hotel.	$5.00 to $7.00.
70 rods.	50	Rockingham House.	$7.00 to $15.00.
5 miles.	20	Saxton's River Hotel.	$7.00.
½ mile.	20	M. H. Ray.	$6.00.
70 rods.	60	Town's Hotel.	$10.50 to $15.00.
		Brandon, Vt.	
80 rods.	100	Brandon Hotel.	$12.00 to $20.00.
8 miles.	200	Lake Dunmore House.	$12.00 to $20.00.
8 miles.	300	Mountain Spring Hotel.	$12.00 to $20.00.
8 miles (P.O., Sudbury).	150	Hyde Manor and Cottages.	$12.00 to $20.00.
10 min. walk.	15	Miss Caroline L. Bishop.	$7.00 to $9.00.
10 min. walk.	4	Misses Estabrook.	$7.00.
½ mile.	4	Mrs. Hiram Blackmer.	$7.00.
3½ miles.	12	Mrs. J. A. Fisk.	$7.00.
½ mile.	14	Mrs. S. W. Jones.	$7.00 to $10.00.
1 mile.	10	Mrs. A. Manchester.	$7.00.
½ mile.	8	Mrs. W. C. Simonds.	$8.00.
2½ miles.	20	Mrs. D. F. H. Pierre.	$8.00.
8 miles.	10	Lyman J. Kelsey.	$7.00.
6 miles.	6	Armon Partlow.	$7.00.
10 miles.	15	Allen J. Mott.	$7.00.
2½ miles.	25	The Alden Cottage.	$5.00.
		Bristol, Vt.	
80 rods.	40	Bristol Hotel.	$2.00 per day. For rate per week apply to J. J. Ridley, Mgr.
80 rods.	40	Commerc'l House.	$2.00 per day. For rate per week apply to R. F. Hatch, Mgr.
		Burlington, Vt.	
½ mile.	75	American House.	$1.25 per day. For rate per week apply to Wither & Read.
¼ mile.	150	Van Ness House.	$10.00 to $20.00.
½ mile.	75	Hotel Burlington.	$8.00 to $15.00.
		Castleton, Vt.	
11 miles from Rutland, 20 rods from Castleton depot.	25	Bomoseen House.	$2.00 per day. For rate per week apply to W. C. Monad.
14 miles from Rutland, 3 miles from Castleton.	25	Lake House.	$1.50 per day. For rate per week apply to H. H. Walker.
14 miles from Rutland, 3 miles from Castleton.	150	Prospect House.	$3.00 per day. For rate per week apply to H. B. Ellis.
		Cavendish, Vt.	
½ mile.	10	Hotel Elliot.	$7.00.
		Charlotte, Vt.	
1½ miles.	25	Eaton Hotel.	$10.00.
1 mile.	10	Lake House.	$8.00 to $10.00.
2 miles.	15	F. Lewis.	$6.00 to $10.00.
		Chester, Vt.	
10 rods.	35	Hotel Chester.	$2.00 per day. For rate per week apply to John Sanborn.
1 mile.	50	The Fullerton.	$2.00 per day. For rate per week apply to Fred Rowell.

Clarendon Springs, Vt.

Distance from Station.	No. of Guests.	Name of Place, Railroad Station.	Rate per Week.
6 miles from Rutland, 2 miles from W. Rutland.	100	Clarendou House.	$2.50 per day. For rate per week apply to G. M. Fletcher.

Cuttingsville, Vt.

¼ mile.	15	Union House.	$5.00.
1¼ miles.	30	The Russell.	$5.00 to $7.00.

Danby, Vt.

100 rods.	30	Danby Hotel.	$7.00 to $15.00.
¼ mile.	3	Mrs. Jas. Fullam.	$5.00 to $7.00.
1 mile.	20	Grand View Terrace.	$5.00 to $7.00.
3 miles.	12	C. D. Kelley.	$6.00 to $8.00.

East Clarendon, Vt.

¼ mile.	8	Maplewood House.	$5.00.
1¼ miles.		H. S. Powers.	$5.00.

East Dorset, Vt.

5 rods.	24	Wilson House.	$7.00 to $10.00.
15 rods.	2	J. L. Cochran.	$6.00.
40 rods.	8	S. Grout.	$6.00.

East Wallingford, Vt.

¼ mile.	6	Cottage Hotel.	$4.00 to $6.00.

Ferrisburgh, Vt.

¼ mile.		Riverside Cottage.	$5.00 to $7.00.
150 rods.	10	C. A. Tupper.	$4.00 to $5.00.
120 rods.	20	Mrs. E. W. Gillette.	$5.00.

Granville, N.Y.

80 rods.	60	Central Hotel.	$2.00 per day. For rate per week apply to D. J. Ructedge.

Hinesburgh, Vt.

12 miles fm. Burlington, 8 miles fm. Shelburne, Vt.	30	Carpenter House.	$2.00 per day. For rate per week apply to C. J. Carpenter.

Keeler's Bay, Vt.

18 miles fm. Burlington, via boat to Gordou's Landing.	30	Iodine Spring House.	$2.00 to $3.00 per day. For rate per week apply to G. W. Squires.
	50	Island House.	For rates apply to Fred Allen.

Lincoln, Vt.

Distance from Station.	No. of Guests.	Name of Place, Railroad Station.	Rate per Week.
5 miles from Bristol, on B. R.R.	25	Lincoln House.	$1.00 per day. For rate per week apply to F. G. Bagley.

Ludlow, Vt.

60 rods.	75	Ludlow House.	$5.00 to $10.00.
90 rods.	50	Goddard House.	$5.00 to $10.00.
6 miles (P.O., Tyson).	100	Echo Lake House.	$7.00 to $10.00.
¼ mile.	6	E. W. Smith.	$4.00 to $6.00.
¼ mile.	6	E. W. Smith.	$4.00 to $6.00.
¼ mile.	6	Mrs. Pauline Chandler.	$4.00 to $6.00.
¼ mile.	6	Mrs. Chas. Fisk.	$4.00 to $6.00.
3 miles (P.O., Tyson).	6	Jas. McDermott.	$4.00 to $6.00.
5 miles " "	6	A. F. Hubbard.	$4.00 to $6.00.
5 miles " "	6	Frank Joslin.	$4.00 to $6.00.
2 miles.	6	Ervin Warren.	$4.00 to $6.00.

Manchester, Vt.

2¼ miles.	300	Equinox House.	$21.00 to $28.00.
2¼ miles.	100	Munson House.	$7.00 to $15.00.
3¼ miles.	30	Summit House.	$7.00 to $15.00.
¼ mile.	80	Colburn House.	$7.00 to $15.00.
¼ mile.	30	Thayer's Hotel.	$7.00 to $15.00.
2 miles.	20	C. L. Randall.	$7.00 to $10.00.
2¼ miles.	30	C. F. Orvis.	$7.00 to $15.00.
¼ mile.	15	R. B. Smith.	$7.00 to $10.00.
¼ mile.	15	A. F. Smith.	$7.00 to $10.00.

Middlebury, Vt.

2 miles.	10	H. Keene.	$1.00 per day.
¼ mile.	75	Addison House.	$10.00 to $15.00.
¼ mile.	30	Logan House.	$2.00 per day. For rate per week apply to J. H. Sargent.
3 miles.	50	Pierce House.	$2.00 per day. For rate per week apply to J. Higgins.
3¼ miles.	10	Glen House.	For rates apply to Frank Farr.
11 miles (P.O., Ripton).	150	Bread Loaf Inn.	$7.00 to $17.00.
7 miles.	50	Mountain View Inn.	$7.00 to $10.00.
¼ mile.	11	Bartlett Hall.	$6.00 to $10.00.
5 miles.	50	Glen House.	$3.00 to $10.00.
3 miles.	4	Pleasant View Farm.	$5.00.
6 miles.	6	A. S. Bingham.	$4.00.
6 miles.	6	Maple Wood Cottage.	$5.00.

Distance from Station.	No. of Guests.	Name of Place, Railroad Station.	Rate per Week.
		Middle Granville, N.Y.	
30 rods.	40	Munson House.	$2.00 per day. For rate per week apply to J. Roll.
		Middletown Springs, Vt.	
15 miles from Rutland, 8 miles from Poultney.	50	Adams House.	$1.50 per day. For rate per week apply to G. D. Adams.
15 miles from Rutland, 8 miles from Poultney.	75	Montvert House.	$1.50 per day. For rate per week apply to J. P. Eager.
15 miles from Rutland, 8 miles from Poultney.	30	Valley House.	$1.50 per day. For rate per week apply to D. A. Barker.
		Mount Holly, Vt.	
2½ miles.	25	Green Mountain Cottage.	$7.00.
¼ mile.	20	The Elms.	$7.00.
		New Haven Jct., Vt.	
¼ mile.	4	Poplar Hill Cottage.	$5.00 to $6.00.
1½ miles.	20	Portch House.	$1.50 per day. For rate per week apply to F. M. Portch.
		North Dorset, Vt.	
25 rods.	10	Mrs. F. R. Allen.	$4.00 to $5.00.
35 rods.	10	G. P. Griffith.	$5.00 to $7.00.
60 rods.	6	Mrs. M. E. Maynard.	$4.00 to $5.00.
¼ mile.	5	Milo Pierce.	$7.00.
		North Ferrisburgh, Vt.	
3½ miles.	12	Frank Louis.	$5.00.
2 miles.	15	P. Dakin.	$4.50.
1 mile.	10	N. L. Kimball.	$5.00.
2 miles.	12	M. L. Richardson.	$5.00.
1½ miles.	15	S. B. Martin.	$7.00.
		Orwell, Vt.	
2½ miles.	50	Eagle Inn.	$4.00 to $15.00.
3 miles.	25	Crammond House.	$6.00 to $10.00.
1½ miles.	8	Mrs. Geo. Thomas.	$6.00 to $8.00.

Distance from Station.	No. of Guests.	Name of Place, Railroad Station.	Rate per Week.
		Pawlet, Vt.	
40 rods.	20	Crescent Valley House.	$3.00 per day. For rate per week apply to E. J. Brown.
40 rods.	30	Franklin House.	$1.50 per day. For rate per week apply to D. W. Bromley.
		Pittsford, Vt.	
1 mile.	40	Mountain View Hotel.	$4.00.
2 miles.	20	Riverside Inn.	$1.50 per day. For rate per week apply to Mrs. J. Poreau.
		Plattsburgh, N.Y.	
¼ mile.	75	Cumberlain Hotel.	$2.50 per day. For rate per week apply to W. C. Randall.
15 rods.	100	Fouquet House.	$2.50 to $4.00. For rate per week apply to P. Smith.
2 miles.	1,000	Hotel Champlain.	$5.00 per day. For rate per week apply to D. Stavey.
		Plymouth, Vt.	
7 miles.	50	Union Hotel.	$1.00 per day. For rate per week apply to L. J. Green.
		Port Henry, N.Y.	
50 rods.	100	Cleveland House.	$2.00 per day. For rate per week apply to J. W. Young.
80 rods.	75	Lee House.	$2.00 per day. For rate per week apply to L. H. Sprague.
		Port Kent, N.Y.	
40 rods.	75	Burough House.	$2.00 per day. For rate per week apply to H. H. Burough.
		Poultney, Vt.	
30 rods.	40	Beamen's Hotel.	$1.50 per day. For rate per week apply to C. C. Beamen.
40 rods.	50	Hotel Poultney.	For rates apply to D. E. O'Brien.
3 miles.	150	Lake View House.	$1.50 per day. For rate per week apply to P. J. Griffith.
2 miles.	40	Oakdale House.	$1.50 per day. For rate per week apply to J. Brown.
		Proctorsville, Vt.	
40 rods.	15	Eagle House.	$7.00.

Distance from Station.	No. of Guests.	Name of Place. Railroad Station.	Rate per Week.
		Rutland, Vt.	
15 rods.	300	Berwick House.	$10.00 to $15.00.
5 rods.	300	Bardwell House.	$10.00 to $15.00.
100 rods.	100	Brock House.	$1.50 per day. For rate per week apply to Sam'l Brock.
75 rods.	75	St. James Hotel.	$1.50 per day. For rate per week apply to E. D. Kennedy.
10 miles.	25	Killington Peak House.	$2.50 per day. For rate per week apply to V. C. Myerhoffer.
		Shelburne, Vt.	
4 miles.	6	Geo. B. Blair.	$7.00.
3½ miles.	6	J. J. Collamer.	$7.00 to $12.00.
3 miles.	6	John Peterson.	$7.00 to $12.00.
2½ miles.	6	Mrs. Sarah M. Peterson.	$7.00 to $12.00.
		Shoreham, Vt.	
4½ miles.	50	Shoreham House.	$1.50 per day. For rate per week apply to H. E. Bissell.
4 miles.	50	United States Htl.	$2.00 per day. For rate per week apply to Mrs. Jas. Farr.
		Springfield, Vt.	
8 miles from Gassett's.	100	Springfield House.	$1.50 per day. For rate per week apply to W. F. Miner.
8 miles from Gassett's.	100	The Adner Brown.	For rates apply to R. D. Downer.
		Ticonderoga, N.Y.	
2 miles.	50	Burleigh House.	$10.00 to $20.00.
2 miles.	50	Hall House.	$5.00 to $7.00
½ mile.	75	Fort 'TI' Hotel.	$7.00 to $12.00.
5 miles.	150	Roger's Rock Hotel.	$7.00 to $12.00.
		Vergennes, Vt.	
¾ mile.	100	Prospect House.	$7.00 to $8.00.
1 mile.	20	American House.	$7.00 to $10.00.
½ mile.	20	Wheeler House	$7.00 to $8.00.
7 miles.	12	Mrs. G. W. Kellogg.	$7.00.
¾ mile.	100	Stevens House.	$9.00 to $12.00.
		Wallingford, Vt.	
50 rods.	100	The New Wallingford.	$8.00 to $15.00.
2 miles.	8	Broad View Farm.	$5.00.
3 miles.	8	Elmhurst.	$5.00.
1 mile.	30	Maple Grove Farm.	$7.00.
2 miles.	8	Mrs. E. R. Green.	$5.00.
		Weathersfield, Vt.	
4 miles from Cavendish.	12	Downer's Hotel.	$7.00.
		Wells, Vt.	
2½ miles from Granville.	50	St. Catherine House.	$2.50 per day. For rate per week apply to Irving Wood.
2½ miles from Granville.	50	Lewis House.	$1.50 per day. For rate per week apply to J. S. Wilcox.
		Weston, Vt.	
8 miles from Chester.	50	Hotel Weston.	For rates apply to R. T. Smith.
		Westport, N.Y.	
½ mile.	100	The Westport.	$2.00 per day. For rate per week apply to E. N. Crawford.
¼ mile.	100	Richard's Hotel.	For rates apply to J. D. Hanks.
		Willsborough, N.Y.	
¼ mile.	50	Green Mountain House.	$2.00 per day. For rate per week apply to E. Brown & Son.
¾ mile.	50	Riverside House.	$2.00 per day. For rate per week apply to Warren Shepard.
		Woodstock, Vt.	
30 miles from Rutland, via stage.	75	Central Hotel.	For rates apply to F. F. Wardwell.
30 miles from Rutland, via stage.	75	Woodstock Inn.	$3.00 per day. For rates per week apply to A. M. Mills.

Summer Excursion Rates to Points on Rutland Railroad.

VIA

New York, New Haven, and Hartford Railroad to Springfield.
Boston and Maine Railroad to South Vernon.
Central Vermont Railroad to Brattleboro'.
Boston and Maine Railroad to Bellows Falls.
Rutland Railroad to Destination.

Return Same Route.

TO		New York.	Stamford, Conn.	South Norwalk, Conn.	Bridgeport, Conn.	New Haven, Conn.	Meriden, Conn.	Middletown, Conn.	New Britain, Conn.	Hartford, Conn.	Greenfield, Mass.	Northampton, Mass.	Holyoke, Mass.	Springfield, Mass.
Bartonsville,	Vermont	$10 00	$8 80	$8 50	$7 90	$7 20	$6 50	$6 50	$6 30	$5 70	. . .	$7 20	$7 45	$7 70
Brandon,	"	11 00	11 00	11 00	10 90	10 20	9 50	9 50	9 30	8 70	$6 20	8 25	8 50	8 75
Brooksville,	"	12 00	12 00	12 00	11 90	11 ?0	10 50	10 50	10 30	9 70	7 25	8 25	8 50	8 75
Burlington,	"	13 50	13 50	13 50	13 40	12 70	12 00	12 00	11 80	11 20	8 70	9 70	9 95	10 20
Centre Rutland,	"	10 25	10 25	10 25	10 15	9 45	8 75	8 75	8 55	7 95	5 45	6 45	6 70	6 95
Charlotte,	"	12 90	12 90	12 90	12 80	12 10	11 40	11 40	11 20	10 60	8 10	9 10	9 35	9 60
Chester,	"	10 15	8 95	8 65	8 05	7 55	6 65	6 65	6 45	5 85	3 40	4 40	4 70	5 10
Cuttingsville,	"	10 15	10 15	10 15	9 55	8 85	8 15	8 15	7 95	7 35	4 85	5 85	6 10	6 35
East Clarendon,	"	10 15	10 15	10 15	9 75	9 05	8 35	8 35	8 15	7 55	5 10	6 10	6 35	6 60
East Wallingford,	"	10 15	10 15	10 00	9 40	8 70	8 00	8 00	7 80	7 20	4 70	5 70	5 95	6 20
Ferrisburg,	"	12 65	12 65	12 65	12 55	11 85	11 15	11 15	10 95	10 35	7 85	8 85	9 10	9 35
Gassetts,	"	10 15	9 15	8 85	8 25	7 55	6 85	6 85	6 65	6 05	3 60	4 60	4 85	5 10
Healdville,	"	10 15	9 90	9 60	9 00	8 30	7 60	7 60	7 40	6 80	4 30	5 30	5 55	5 80
Leicester Junction,	"	11 25	11 25	11 25	11 15	10 45	9 75	9 75	9 55	8 95	6 45	7 45	7 70	7 95
Ludlow,	"	10 15	9 65	9 35	8 75	8 05	7 35	7 35	7 15	6 55	4 05	5 05	5 30	5 55
Middlebury,	"	11 80	11 80	11 80	11 70	11 00	10 30	10 30	10 10	9 50	7 00	8 00	8 25	8 50
Mt. Holly,	"	10 15	10 15	9 85	9 25	8 55	7 85	7 85	7 65	7 05	4 55	5 55	5 80	6 05
New Haven Junction,	"	12 25	12 25	12 25	12 15	11 45	10 75	10 75	10 55	9 95	7 45	8 45	8 70	8 95
North Clarendon,	"	10 15	10 15	10 15	9 90	9 20	8 50	8 50	8 30	7 70	5 25	6 25	6 50	6 75
North Ferrisburg,	"	12 75	12 75	12 75	12 65	11 95	11 25	11 25	11 05	10 45	8 00	9 00	9 25	9 50
Orwell,	"	11 75	11 75	11 75	11 65	10 95	10 25	10 25	10 05	9 45	6 95	7 95	8 20	8 45
Pittsford,	"	10 65	10 65	10 65	10 55	9 85	9 15	9 15	8 95	8 35	5 85	6 85	7 10	7 35
Proctor,	"	10 50	10 50	10 50	10 40	9 70	9 00	9 00	8 80	8 20	5 70	6 70	6 95	7 20
Proctorsville,	"	10 15	9 45	9 15	8 55	7 85	7 15	7 15	6 95	6 35	3 85	4 85	5 15	5 40
Rockingham,	"	9 75	8 55	8 25	7 65	6 95	6 25	6 25	6 05	5 45				
Rutland,	"	10 15	10 15	10 15	10 05	9 35	8 65	8 65	8 45	7 85	5 35	6 35	6 60	6 85
Salisbury,	"	11 50	11 50	11 50	11 40	10 70	10 00	10 00	9 80	9 20	6 70	7 70	7 95	8 20
Shelburne,	"	13 15	13 15	13 15	13 05	12 35	11 65	11 65	11 45	10 85	8 40	9 40	9 70	10 00
Shoreham,	"	11 55	11 55	11 55	11 45	10 75	10 05	10 05	9 85	9 25	6 75	7 75	8 00	8 25
Summit,	"	10 15	9 95	9 65	9 05	8 35	7 65	7 65	7 45	6 85	4 45	5 45	5 70	5 95
Ticonderoga, N.Y. (Addison Junct.)		12 05	12 05	12 05	12 00	11 30	10 60	10 60	10 40	9 80	7 25	8 25	8 50	8 75
Vergennes, Vermont		12 50	12 50	12 50	12 40	11 70	11 00	11 00	10 80	10 20	7 70	8 70	8 95	9 20
Whiting,	"	11 40	11 40	11 40	11 30	10 60	9 90	9 90	9 70	9 10	6 60	7 60	7 85	8 10

Summer Excursion Rates to Points on Rutland Railroad.

(138)

TO	VIA Fitchburg Railroad to Bellows Falls. Rutland Railroad to Destination. Return Same Route. FROM			From Stations on Line of New York, New Haven, & Hartford Railroad (Old Colony System) via Boston or Fitchburg, unless otherwise noted. Return Same Route. FROM										
	Boston, Mass.	Fitchburg, Mass.	Worcester, Mass.	Fall River, Mass.	Mansfield, Mass.	New Bedford, Mass.	Newport, R.I.	Pawtucket, R.I., via Worcester.	Pawtucket, R.I.	Providence, R.I., via Worcester.	Providence, R.I.	South Framingham, Mass.	Taunton, Mass.	Woonsocket, R.I.
Bartonsville, Vt.	$5 10			$7 20	$6 10	$7 40	$7 60	$5 60	$6 70	$5 75	$6 85	$5 10	$6 60	$5 40
Brandon, "	8 10	$7 00	$7 00	10 20	9 10	10 40	10 60	8 60	9 70	8 75	9 85	8 10	9 60	8 40
Brooksville, "	9 20	8 10	8 10	11 30	10 20	11 50	11 70	9 70	10 80	9 85	10 95	9 20	10 70	9 50
Burlington, "	10 50	9 50	9 50	12 60	11 50	12 80	13 00	11 10	12 10	11 25	12 25	10 50	12 00	10 90
Cavendish, "	5 70	4 70	4 70	7 80	6 70	8 00	8 20	6 20	7 30	6 35	7 45	5 70	7 20	6 00
Centre Rutland, "	7 35	6 25	6 25	9 45	8 35	9 65	9 85	7 85	8 95	8 00	9 10	7 35	8 85	7 65
Charlotte, "	10 00	8 90	8 90	12 10	11 00	12 30	12 50	10 50	11 60	10 65	11 75	10 00	11 50	10 30
Chester, "	5 25	4 25	4 25	7 55	6 25	7 55	7 75	5 75	6 85	5 90	7 00	5 25	6 75	5 55
Cuttingsville, "	6 75	5 65	5 65	8 85	7 75	9 05	9 25	7 25	8 35	7 40	8 50	6 75	8 25	7 05
East Clarendon, "	6 95	5 85	5 85	9 05	7 95	9 25	9 45	7 45	8 55	7 60	8 70	6 95	8 45	7 25
East Wallingford, "	6 60	5 50	5 50	8 70	7 60	8 90	9 10	7 10	8 20	7 25	8 35	6 60	8 10	6 90
Ferrisburg, "	9 70	8 60	8 60	11 85	10 75	12 05	12 25	10 25	11 35	10 40	11 50	9 75	11 25	10 05
Gassetts, "	5 45	4 45	4 45	7 55	6 45	7 75	7 95	5 95	7 05	6 10	7 20	5 45	6 95	5 75
Healdville, "	6 20	5 10	5 10	8 30	7 20	8 50	8 70	6 70	7 80	6 85	7 95	6 20	7 70	6 50
Leicester Junction, "	8 35	7 25	7 25	10 45	9 35	10 65	10 85	8 85	9 95	9 00	10 10	8 35	9 85	8 65
Ludlow, "	5 95	4 85	4 85	8 05	6 95	8 25	8 45	6 45	7 55	6 60	7 70	5 95	7 45	6 25
Middlebury, "	8 95	7 85	7 85	11 05	9 95	11 25	11 45	9 45	10 55	9 60	10 70	8 95	10 45	9 25
Mount Holly, "	6 45	5 35	5 35	8 55	7 45	8 75	8 95	6 95	8 05	7 10	8 20	6 45	7 95	6 75
New Haven Junct., "	9 35	8 25	8 25	11 45	10 35	11 65	11 85	9 85	10 95	10 00	11 10	9 35	10 85	9 65
North Clarendon, "	7 10	6 00	6 00	9 20	8 10	9 40	9 60	7 60	8 70	7 75	8 85	7 10	8 60	7 40
North Ferrisburg, "	9 85	8 75	8 75	11 95	10 85	12 15	12 35	10 35	11 45	10 50	11 60	9 85	11 35	10 15
Orwell, "	8 85	7 75	7 75	10 95	9 85	11 15	11 35	9 35	10 45	9 50	10 60	8 85	10 35	9 15
Pittsford, "	7 75	6 65	6 65	9 85	8 75	10 05	10 25	8 25	9 35	8 40	9 50	7 75	9 25	8 05
Proctor, "	7 60	6 50	6 50	9 70	8 60	9 90	10 10	8 10	9 20	8 25	9 35	7 60	9 10	7 90
Proctorsville, "	5 75	4 65	4 65	7 85	6 75	8 05	8 25	6 25	7 35	6 40	7 50	5 75	7 25	6 05
Rockingham.	4 85	3 85	3 85											
Rutland, "	7 25	6 15	6 15	9 35	8 25	9 55	9 75	7 75	8 85	7 90	9 00	7 25	8 75	7 55
Rutland Valley, "	7 50	6 40	6 40											
Salisbury, "	8 60	7 50	7 50	10 70	9 60	10 90	11 10	9 10	10 20	9 25	10 35	8 60	10 10	8 90
Shelburne, "	10 25	9 15	9 15	12 35	11 25	12 55	12 75	10 75	11 85	10 90	12 00	10 25	11 75	10 55
Shoreham, "	8 70	7 60	7 60	10 80	9 70	11 00	11 20	9 20	10 30	9 35	10 45	8 70	10 20	8 90
Summit, "	6 25	5 15	5 15	8 45	7 35	8 65	8 85	6 85	7 95	7 00	8 10	6 35	7 85	6 65
Ticonderoga, N. Y. (Addison Junction)	9 20	8 10	8 10	11 30	10 20	11 50	11 70	9 70	10 80	9 85	10 95	9 20	10 70	9 50
Vergennes, Vt.	9 60	8 50	8 50	11 70	10 60	11 90	12 10	10 10	11 20	10 25	11 35	9 60	11 10	9 90
Whiting, "	8 50	7 40	7 40	10 60	9 50	10 80	11 00	9 00	10 10	9 15	10 25	8 50	10 00	8 80

Summary Tourist Rates.

—

From New York.

To Montreal via Rutland and Burlington.
Sound Lines to Boston.
Transfer.
Fitchburg R R. to Bellows Falls.
Rutland R.R. to Burlington.
Central Vt. R.R. to St. Johns.
Grand Trunk Ry. to Montreal.
Return same route.

Rate, $24.10.

Via Rutland, Burlington, and Lake Champlain.
Sound Lines to Boston.
Transfer.
Fitchburg R.R. to Bellows Falls.
Rutland R.R. to Burlington.
Champlain Transportation Co. to Plattsburgh.
Delaware & Hudson R.R. to Rouse's Point.
Grand Trunk Ry. to Montreal.
Return same route.

Rate, $24.65.

Via Rutland, Burlington, and Lake Champlain.
Sound Lines to Boston.
Transfer.
Fitchburg R.R. to Bellows Falls.
Rutland R.R. to Burlington.
Champlain Transportation Co. to Plattsburgh.
Delaware & Hudson R.R. to Rouse's Point.
Grand Trunk Ry. to Montreal.
Grand Trunk Ry. to St. John.
Central Vermont R.R. to Burlington.
Rutland R.R. to Bellows Falls.
Fitchburg R.R. to Boston.
Transfer.
Sound Lines to New York.

Rate, $25.90. This route may be reversed between Burlington and Montreal, if desired.

To Plattsburgh (Bluff Point), Hotel Champlain, via Burlington and Lake Champlain.
Sound Lines to Boston.
Transfer.
Fitchburg R.R. to Bellows Falls.
Rutland R.R. to Burlington.
Champlain Transportation Co. to Plattsburgh (Bluff Point).
Return same route.

Rate, $20.65.

Via Ticonderoga.

Sound Lines to Boston.
Transfer.
Fitchburg R.R. to Bellows Falls.
Rutland R.R. to Ticonderoga (Addison Jct.).
D. & H. R.R. to Plattsburgh (Bluff Point).
Return same route.

Rate, $20.85.

To Lake George (Caldwell) via Ticonderoga.
Sound Lines to Boston.
Transfer.
Fitchburg R.R. to Bellows Falls.
Rutland R.R. to Ticonderoga (Addison Jct.).
D. & H. R.R. to Lake George (Caldwell).
Return same route.

Rate, $20.65.

To Lake George (Caldwell) via Ticonderoga. Return via Albany.
Sound Lines to Boston.
Transfer.
Fitchburg R.R. to Bellows Falls.
Rutland R.R. to Ticonderoga (Addison Jct.).
D. & H. R.R. to Baldwin
Lake George Steamboat Co. to Caldwell.
Delaware & Hudson R.R. to Albany.
Night Line Steamers to New York.

Rate, $16.65.

To Burlington, Vt., via Rutland. Return via White Mountains.
Sound Lines to Boston.
Transfer.

(184)

Fitchburg R.R. to Bellows Falls.
Rutland R.R. to Burlington.
Central Vt. R.R. to Cambridge Jct.
St. John & L.C. R.R. to Lunenburg.
Maine Central Ry. to North Conway.
Boston & Maine R.R. to Boston.
Transfer.
Sound Lines to New York.

Rate, $23.65.

To Montreal via Rutland and Burlington. Return via Newport, Vt.

Sound Lines to Boston.
Transfer.
Fitchburg R.R. to Bellows Falls.
Rutland R.R. to Burlington.
Central Vt. R.R. to St. Johns.
Grand Trunk Ry. to Montreal.
Canadian Pacific Ry. to Newport.
Boston & Maine R.R. to Boston.
Transfer.
Sound Lines to New York.

Rate, $27.00.

To Montreal via Rutland and Burlington. Return via White Mountains.

Sound Lines to Boston.
Transfer.
Fitchburg R.R. to Bellows Falls.
Rutland R.R. to Burlington.
Central Vt. R.R. to St. Johns.
Grand Trunk Ry. to Montreal.
Canadian Pacific Ry. to Newport.
Boston & Maine R.R. to St. Johnsbury.
St. Johnsbury & L.C. R.R. to Lunenburg.
Maine Central R.R. to North Conway.
Boston & Maine R.R. to Boston.
Transfer.
Sound Lines to New York.

Rate, $27.00.

To Ottawa via Rutland, Burlington, and Rouse's Point.

Sound Lines to Boston.
Transfer.
Fitchburg R.R. to Bellows Falls.
Rutland R.R. to Burlington.
Central Vt. R.R. to Rouse's Point.
Canada Atlantic Ry. to Ottawa.
Return same route.

Rate, $27.00.

To Quebec via Rutland, Burlington, and Montreal.

Sound Lines to Boston.
Transfer.
Fitchburg R.R. to Bellows Falls.
Rutland R.R. to Burlington.
Central Vt. R.R. to Montreal.
Grand Trunk Ry. to Montreal.
Grand Trunk Ry. to Quebec.
Return same route.

Rate, $27.80.

To New York via Rutland and Saratoga.

Sound Lines to Boston.
Transfer.
Fitchburg R.R. to Bellows Falls.
Rutland R.R. to Rutland.
Delaware & Hudson R.R. to Albany.
Day Line Steamers to New York.

Rate, $12.25.

To New York via Rutland and Burlington.

Sound Lines to Boston.
Transfer.
Fitchburg R.R. to Bellows Falls.
Rutland R.R. to Burlington.
Champlain Transportation Co. to Fort Ticon-
deroga.
Delaware & Hudson R.R. to Baldwin.
Lake George Steamboat Co. to Caldwell.
Delaware & Hudson R.R. to Albany.
Day Line Steamers to New York.

Rate, $19.55.

To New York via Rutland.

Sound Lines to Boston.
Transfer.
Fitchburg R.R. to Bellows Falls.
Rutland R.R. to Rutland.
Bennington & Rutland Ry. to White Creek.
Fitchburg R.R. to Troy.
Delaware & Hudson R.R. to Albany.
Day Line Steamers to New York.

Rate, $12.25.

To New York via Burlington.

Day Line Steamers to Albany.
D. & H. R.R. to Troy.
Fitchburg R.R. to White Creek.
Bennington & Rutland Ry. to Rutland.
Rutland R.R. to Burlington.
Champlain Transportation Co. to Fort Ticon-
deroga.
Delaware & Hudson R.R. to Albany.
Day Line Steamers to New York.

Rate, $12.80. This route may be reversed,
if desired.

To Burlington, Vt., and return.

Day Line Steamers to Albany.
Delaware & Hudson R.R. to Troy.
Fitchburg R.R. to White Creek.
Bennington & Rutland Ry. to Rutland.
Rutland R.R. to Burlington.
Return same route.

Rate, $12.00.

To Montreal, P.Q.

Day Line Steamers to Albany.
Delaware & Hudson R.R. to Troy.
Fitchburg R.R. to White Creek.
Bennington & Rutland Ry. to Rutland.
Rutland R.R. to Burlington.
Central Vt. R.R. to St. Johns.
Grand Trunk R.R. to Montreal.
Return same route.

Rate, $14.05.

(185)

**To Montreal, P.Q., via Burlington. Return via
Lakes Champlain and George.**

Day Line Steamers to Albany.
Delaware & Hudson R.R. to Troy.
Fitchburg R.R. to White Creek.
Bennington & Rutland Ry. to Rutland.
Rutland R.R. to Burlington.
Central Vt. R.R. to St. Johns.
Grand Trunk Ry. to Montreal.
Grand Trunk Ry. to Rouse's Point.
Delaware & Hudson R.R. to Plattsburgh.
Champlain Transportation Co. to Fort Ticon-
deroga.
Delaware & Hudson R.R. to Baldwin.
Lake George Steamers to Caldwell.
Delaware & Hudson R.R. to Troy.
N.Y.C. & H. R.R. to New York.

Rate, $20.50.

—

From Boston.

To Manchester, Vt., via Rutland.

Fitchburg R.R. to Bellows Falls.
Rutland R.R. to Rutland.
Bennington & Rutland Ry. to Manchester.
Return same route.

Rate, $9.05.

**To Ausable Chasm via Burlington. Return via
Lakes Champlain and George.**

Fitchburg R.R. to Bellows Falls.
Rutland R.R. to Burlington.
Champlain Transportation Co. to Port Kent.
K.A.C. & L.C. R.R. to Ausable Chasm.
K.A.C. & L.C. R.R. to Port Kent.
Champlain Transportation Co. to Fort Ticon-
deroga.
Delaware & Hudson R.R. to Baldwin.
Lake George Steamers to Caldwell.
Delaware & Hudson R.R. to Saratoga.
Fitchburg R.R. to Boston.

Rate, $17.25.

To Local Points on Chateaugay R.R.
Fitchburg R.R. to Bellows Falls.
Rutland R.R. to Burlington.
Champlain Transportation Co. to Plattsburgh.
Chateaugay R.R. to points named:
Return same route.
  Chazy Lake, N.Y., $14.15.
  Lyon Mountain, $14.50.
  Loon Lake, $15.35.
  Bloomingdale, $15.35.
  Saranac Lake, $15.85.

To Plattsburgh (Bluff Point), Hotel Champlain.
Fitchburg R.R. to Bellows Falls.
Rutland R.R. to Burlington.
Champlain Transportation Co. to Plattsburgh (Bluff Point).
Return same route.
  Rate, $11.85.

To Lake Placid.
Fitchburg R.R. to Bellows Falls.
Rutland R.R. to Burlington.
Champlain Transportation Co. to Plattsburgh.
Chateaugay R.R. to Saranac Lake.
Saranac & Lake Placid R.R. to Lake Placid.
Return same route.
  Rate, $17.10.

To Loon Lake House.
Fitchburg R.R. to Bellows Falls.
Rutland R.R. to Burlington.
Champlain Trans. Co. to Plattsburgh.
Chateaugay R.R. to Loon Lake Station.
Stage to Loon Lake House.
Return same route.
  Rate, $16.85.

To Paul Smith's, N.Y.
Fitchburg R.R. to Bellows Falls.
Rutland R.R. to Burlington.
Central Vermont R.R. to Moira.
Northern New York R.R. to Paul Smith's.
Return same route.
  Rate, $16.85.

To Ralph's (Upper Chateaugay Lake).
Fitchburg R.R. to Bellows Falls.
Rutland R.R. to Burlington.
Champlain Trans. Co. to Plattsburgh.
Chateaugay R.R. to Lyon Mountain.
Stage to Ralph's.
Return same route.
  Rate, $15.50.

To Saranac Inn.
Fitchburg R.R. to Bellows Falls.
Rutland R.R. to Burlington.
Champlain Trans. Co. to Plattsburgh.
Chateaugay R.R. to Saranac Lake.
Saranac Inn Stage Co. to Saranac Inn.
Return same route.
  Rate, $16.85.

To Saratoga, N.Y.
Fitchburg R.R. to Bellows Falls.
Rutland R.R. to Rutland.
Delaware & Hudson R.R. to Saratoga.
Return same route.
  Rate, $10.00.

To Saratoga, N.Y.
Fitchburg R.R. to Bellows Falls.
Rutland R.R. to Rutland.
Delaware & Hudson R.R. to Saratoga.
Delaware & Hudson R.R. to Albany.
Day Line Steamers to New York.
Sound Lines to Boston.
  Rate, $13.25.

To Saratoga, N.Y.
Fitchburg R.R. to Bellows Falls.
Rutland R.R. to Rutland.
Delaware & Hudson R.R. to Saratoga.
Delaware & Hudson R.R. to Albany.
W.S. R.R. or N.Y.C. R.R. to New York.
Sound Lines to Boston.
  Rate, $14.25.

To Saratoga, N.Y.
Fitchburg R.R. to Bellows Falls.
Rutland R.R. to Burlington.
Champlain Trans. Co. to Fort Ticonderoga.
Delaware & Hudson R.R. to Baldwin.
Lake George Steamers to Caldwell.
Delaware & Hudson R.R. to Saratoga.
Hoosac Tunnel Route to Boston.
  Rate, $16.50.

To Montreal.
Fitchburg R.R. to Bellows Falls.
Rutland R.R. to Burlington.
Central Vt. R.R. to St. Johns.
Grand Trunk Ry. to Montreal.
Return same route.
  Rate, $15.10.

To Montreal via Rutland & Burlington. Return via Newport, Vt.
Fitchburg R.R. to Bellows Falls.
Rutland R.R. to Burlington.
Central Vt. R.R. to St. Johns.
Grand Trunk Ry. to Montreal.
Canadian Pacific Ry. to Newport.
Boston & Maine R.R. to Boston.
  Rate, $18.00.

To Montreal via Rutland & Burlington. Return via White Mountains.
Fitchburg R.R. to Bellows Falls.
Rutland R.R. to Burlington.
Central Vt. R.R. to St. Johns.
Grand Trunk Ry. to Montreal.
Canadian Pacific Ry. to Newport.
Boston & Maine R.R. to St. Johnsbury.
St. Johnsbury & Lake Champlain R.R. to Lunenburg.
Maine Central R.R. to North Conway.
Boston & Maine R.R. to Boston.
  Rate, $18.00.

To Montreal via Burlington. Return via Lakes Champlain and George, and Saratoga.

Fitchburg R.R. to Bellows Falls.
Rutland R.R. to Burlington.
Central Vt. R.R. to St. Johns.
Grand Trunk Ry. to Montreal.
Grand Trunk Ry. to Rouse's Point.
Delaware & Hudson R.R. to Plattsburgh.
Champlain Trans. Co. to Fort Ticonderoga.
Delaware & Hudson R.R. to Baldwin.
Lake George Steamers to Caldwell.
Delaware & Hudson R.R. to Saratoga.
Hoosac Tunnel Route to Boston.

Rate, $22.15.

To Montreal via Burlington. Return via Lake Champlain and Saratoga.

Fitchburg R.R. to Bellows Falls.
Rutland R.R. to Burlington.
Central Vt. R.R. to St. Johns.
Grand Trunk Ry. to Montreal.
Grand Trunk Ry. to Rouse's Point.
Delaware & Hudson R.R. to Plattsburgh.
Champlain Trans. Co. to Fort Ticonderoga.
Delaware & Hudson R.R. to Saratoga.
Hoosac Tunnel Route to Boston.

Rate, $20.65.

To Montreal via Rutland and Burlington. Return via Niagara Falls and Saratoga.

Fitchburg R.R. to Bellows Falls.
Rutland R.R. to Burlington.
Central Vt. R.R. to St. Johns.
Grand Trunk Ry. to Montreal.
Grand Trunk Ry. to Toronto.
Niagara Navigation Co. to Lewiston.
N.Y.C. & H. R.R. to Niagara Falls.
W.S. R.R. to Rotterdam.
Hoosac Tunnel Route to Boston. Direct or via Saratoga, at option of purchaser.

Rate, $30.40.

To Ottawa via Rutland, Burlington, and Rouse's Point.

Fitchburg R.R. to Bellows Falls.
Rutland R.R. to Burlington.
Central Vt. R.R. to Rouse's Point.
Canada Atlantic Ry. to Ottawa.
Return same route.

Rate, $18.00.

To Quebec via Rutland, Burlington, and Montreal.

Fitchburg R.R. to Bellows Falls.
Rutland R.R. to Burlington.
Central Vt. R.R. to St. Johns.
Grand Trunk Ry. to Montreal.
Grand Trunk Ry. to Quebec.
Return same route.

Rate, $18.90.

To Montreal via Rutland, Burlington, and Lake Champlain.

Fitchburg R.R. to Bellows Falls.
Rutland R.R. to Burlington.
Champlain Trans. Co. to Plattsburgh.
Delaware & Hudson R.R. to Rouse's Point.
Grand Trunk Ry. to Montreal.
Return same route.

Rate, $15.65.

To Montreal via Rutland, Burlington, and Lake Champlain.

Fitchburg R.R. to Bellows Falls.
Rutland R.R. to Burlington.
Champlain Trans. Co. to Plattsburgh.
Delaware & Hudson R.R. to Rouse's Point.
Grand Trunk Ry. to Montreal.
Grand Trunk Ry. to St. Johns.
Central Vt. R.R. to Burlington.
Rutland R.R. to Bellows Falls.
Fitchburg R.R. to Boston.

Rate, $16.90. This route may be reversed between Burlington and Montreal, if desired.

(187)

To Plattsburgh (Bluff Point), Hotel Champlain, via Ticonderoga.

Fitchburg R.R. to Bellows Falls.
Rutland R.R. to Ticonderoga (Addison Jct.).
Delaware & Hudson R.R. to Plattsburgh (Bluff Point).
Return same route.

Rate, $11.85.

To Lake George (Caldwell) via Ticonderoga.

Fitchburg R.R. to Bellows Falls.
Rutland R.R. to Ticonderoga (Addison Jct.).
Delaware & Hudson R.R. to Lake George (Caldwell).
Return same route.

Rate, $11.65.

To Burlington, Vt., via Rutland. Return via White Mountains.

Fitchburg R.R. to Bellows Falls.
Rutland R.R. to Burlington.
Central Vt. R.R. to Cambridge Junction.
St. Johnsbury & Lake Champlain R.R. to Lunenburg.
Maine Central R.R. to North Conway.
Boston & Maine R.R. to Boston.

Rate, $14.65.

To Local Points on the Delaware & Hudson R.R.

Fitchburg R.R. to Bellows Falls.
Rutland R.R. to Rutland.
Delaware & Hudson R.R. to destination.
Return same route.

Castleton	$7 90	Port Henry	$11 10
Poultney	8 30	Baldwin	11 50
Middle Granville	8 75	Westport	11 25
Granville	8 85	Port Kent	11 25
Whitehall	8 80	Plattsburgh	11 85
Ticonderoga	10 60	Ausable	13 05
Crown Point	10 60		

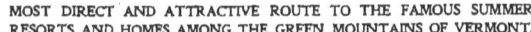

LAKE CHAMPLAIN ❧

❧ AND LAKE GEORGE.

"The Gateway of the Country."

THIS ROUTE OFFERS ATTRACTIONS TO THE
PLEASURE SEEKERS UNSURPASSED BY THOSE
OF ANY LINE OF SUMMER TRAVEL . . . .

❦ ❦ ❦ ❦ ❦

Elegant and commodious steamers pass in sight of some of the
grandest scenery and most noted historical points in America, and with
rail and stage connections give the tourist an opportunity to visit the
Forests, Streams, Lakes and Mountains of this famous region.

Main and close connections with D. & H. C. Co.'s R. R. for all
points North, South and West; with Chateaugay R. R. for Adirondack
Mountains; with Central Vermont R. R., for White Mountains, and with
Central Vermont and Rutland R. Rs. for all resorts in New England.

FOR TIME TABLES, MAPS, AND
ILLUSTRATED GUIDE BOOK, ADDRESS ❧

GEORGE RUSHLOW,
General Manager.

General Office, BURLINGTON, VT.

The Massachusetts
Mutual Life Insurance Company,

SPRINGFIELD, MASS.

JOHN A. HALL, President.   Incorporated 1851.   HENRY M. PHILLIPS, Sec'y.

* * * * * * * * *

...A COMPARISON OF FIVE YEARS...

	1891.	1896.	Gains.	Percentage of Gains.
Premium Income	$2,393,103.88	$3,610,768.70	$1,217,664.82	50.9
Income from Interest, Rents, etc.	558,597.97	801,199.13	242,601.16	43.4
Total	2,951,701.85	4,411,967.83	1,460,265.98	49.5
Assets	12,239,529.16	18,546,959.96	6,307,430.80	51.5
Insurance in force	25,010 policies insuring	40,926 policies insuring	15,916 policies insuring	
	$69,527,665.00	$102,867,061.00	$33,339,396.00	48.0

* * * * * * * * *

Since its organization the MASSACHUSETTS MUTUAL LIFE INSURANCE COMPANY has paid to policy holders

In death claims $15,110,723.77
Endowments matured . . 2,578,826.00
Dividends 7,174,696.98

Assets, December 31, 1896, $18,546,959.96   Liabilities, $17,205,296.32   Surplus, $1,341,663.64

vi

vii

viii

The Brandon Inn.

A FIRST-CLASS HOTEL WITH EVERY MODERN CONVENIENCE, OPEN THROUGHOUT THE YEAR.
SPECIAL ATTENTION GIVEN TO SUMMER BUSINESS.

For terms, with particulars, apply to
SHOFF & SALTER, Prop's, BRANDON, VT.

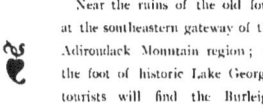
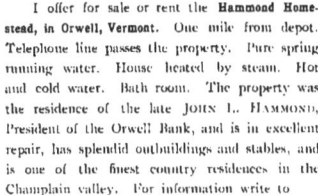

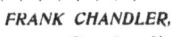

xiii

HYDE MANOR and Lake Hortonia

HYDE MANOR is one of the most attractive of the Northern Summer Resorts, and is particularly recommended to the attention of those who desire a pleasant family home during the heated period. For illustrated circular, address A. W. HYDE, Sudbury, Vt.

MOUNTAIN VIEW INN,

... T. W. FLETCHER, Prop'r ...

BRIDPORT, VERMONT.

* * *

... TERMS ...

The terms are $7 to $10 per week. Special arrangements will be made for families or persons making a prolonged stay. References are required and given in all cases. Hebrews will not be taken as guests. Address all telegrams to **Mountain View Inn**, care of CHAPMAN & CO., Middlebury, Vt. Write for circular.

TELEPHONE CONNECTION WITH MIDDLEBURY.

THE ADDISON HOUSE   H. E. BISSELL, .. Proprietor ..   Middlebury, Vt.

* * * * * *

This Hotel is situated in "the prettiest village in New England," and has a commanding location. The house has been newly remodelled and refurnished throughout, is steam heated, has hot and cold water baths on every floor, and has ample accommodations for **150** guests. Its cuisine is not surpassed, and in fact it is just the place where summer visitors will find a pleasant home.

The beautiful Otter runs winding through the heart of the village. There are fine stretches for rowing, excellent fishing, good hunting in the season, and splendid drives in and around the town, with numerous places of historic interest, and much picturesque and magnificent scenery within easy distances.

The Addison is faced on two sides by beautiful and shady parks, and its grounds embrace spacious croquet and tennis courts. The post office is within two minutes' walk and the railroad station within five minutes' walk of the hotel, while there are telegraph and telephone offices in the house.

Connected with the house is a well-equipped livery, where elegant turnouts may be obtained on reasonable terms.

Rates. — For rates, descriptive pamphlets, etc., address the proprietor.

XVI.

NOTHING APPEALS TO THE ARTISTIC EYE
LIKE ARTISTIC CEMETERY WORK . . . .

❤ ❤ ❤

For ages, events and periods in history, and great men, have been immortalized in stone: then why should we not perpetuate the memory of our own?

 WE DEAL DIRECT WITH
THE CONSUMER . . . . . .

Anything In
Stone. GRANITE and
MARBLE.

EVERSON & CO.,
Rutland, Vt.